Jillian Cade

FAKE →paranormal
investigator

Jillian Cade

FAKE → paranormal investigator

JEN KLEIN

Published in the United States by Soho Teen
an imprint of
Soho Press, Inc.
853 Broadway
New York, NY 10003

Library of Congress Cataloging-in-Publication Data

Klein, Jen.
Jillian Cade : (fake) paranormal investigator / Jen Klein.

ISBN 978-1-61695-690-5
eISBN 978-1-61695-435-2

1. Supernatural—Fiction. 2. Mystery and detective stories. 3. Missing persons—Fiction. 4. Love—Fiction. I. Title.
PZ7.1.K645Ji 2015 [Fic]—dc23 2015009888

Interior design by Janine Agro, Soho Press, Inc.

Printed in the United States of America

10 9 8 7 6 5 4 3 2 1

For
Jeana and Ellie and Anna

Jillian Cade

FAKE → paranormal
investigator

ONE

On the rare occasion that I meet a new guy, he inevitably has one of two reactions: he wants to save me or screw me. Since I'm not up for either, I don't get asked on a lot of second dates.

Technically speaking, none.

This only partially explained why, at eleven thirty on a Saturday night, I was huddled on the floor of a dark hallway between my cousin Norbert and a middle-aged whack job named Paula.

"Is it time?" the whack job whispered.

I didn't know, but it didn't matter. "Four minutes," I said.

Whack Job Paula gestured around us. "It's a beautiful house, right?"

I glanced up. From where I was squatting, I could barely make out a polished wooden floor and two walls. "Sure."

"It's a Craftsman," she said. "Built in 1902."

"That explains the ghosts." I used the most official voice I could muster. "Hauntings almost never occur in newer houses."

Beside me, Norbert nodded. "It's true," he confirmed. It was shocking that his scrawny neck could hold his head upright, weighted down as it was under a giant set of headphones. I happened to know that the phones were picking up exactly nothing, but Paula didn't need that information.

"Got anything?" I asked Norbert.

He fiddled with the rectangular object at his waist. It was a defunct VCR remote that I had spray-painted black and hot-glued to an old phone cord: also filed under the heading *Paula Doesn't Need to Know.* "Nothing yet. Time check?"

"Three minutes," I answered.

"It always happens at eleven thirty-four P.M.," said Paula. "Every night since moving in." We had been over this several times, but Paula seemed to like the sound of her own voice. "I go to sleep early because I'm a teacher, but then I wake up right at eleven thirty-four."

God help the children of America.

Paula took a sip from the glass at her side. She had offered some to us earlier, but Norbert and I had both politely explained that we don't drink on the job. Apparently Paula was such a dingdong that it didn't occur to her not to serve alcohol to minors. It was true that, with the right accoutrements, I could pass for older than my seventeen years, but Norbert looked exactly like what he was: a new high school freshman.

"Even though I turn off the light before going to bed, it's always back on. And when I come out here"—Paula's voice lowered like she was telling ghost stories around a Girl Scout campfire instead of on her hallway floor—"I can feel a *presence.*"

I felt Norbert tense up. Two minutes.

"I turn off the hallway light," Paula continued. "And as I'm heading back toward my room, I hear a scratching. It doesn't come from any one place. I can hear it all around me. It's like something is trying to claw down the divide between dimensions—through the wall between the living and the dead."

Norbert edged closer to me. I resisted the urge to pinch the back of his neck and scare the crap out of him. An epic Norbert freak-out would be hilarious, but then Paula might realize we were two kids who were conning her and not legitimate paranormal investigators (an oxymoron if there ever was one). "There's a Chumash grave site up the road," I whispered. "I bet some of their spirits were restless and wandered in this direction. It happens all the time."

Actually, it happens *never*. But if Paula knew that, I wouldn't have money for frozen pizzas.

I held up a finger. One minute. Very subtly, I reached into my pocket for the battery-operated metronome I had wrapped in tinfoil. I pressed a button on the side and started to slowly turn the volume up from zero. It took a second before the sound registered in my ears.

Paula lifted her head. "What's that?"

"The detection system," I explained in a low voice. "We're getting something."

Norbert was statue still. He appeared to be listening just as hard as Paula. I stabbed him in the ribs with my finger. "Ow!" he yelped.

"Ow what?" asked Paula.

I stabbed him again. "My—ow!—my butt fell asleep," said Norbert. He fiddled with the VCR remote. "Electro-magnetic emissions are increasing."

"So it's real," breathed Paula. "I'm not crazy."

"Not at all," I lied, turning up the metronome.

Tick. Tick. Tick.

We all waited. The hallway lights stayed off. No scratching could be heard. My right foot started to cramp in a big way. I tried to flex, but that only seemed to make it worse. The muscle in my arch tightened, and I felt my toes curling downward. I shifted, attempting to straighten my leg, and accidentally kneed Norbert in the hip. A deafening electronic scream blasted from his pants.

Paula jumped; Norbert horror-movie shrieked; and I leapt to my feet, momentarily forgetting about my arch cramp. With my right foot trying to turn itself into a fist, I lost my balance and staggered into the wall, then fell back down onto Norbert's lap. Thankfully, my ass must have landed on the key-chain alarm he inexplicably carries, because the sound died immediately.

Paula broke the silence. "What the hell?"

Norbert opened his mouth, but I jumped in before he could screw it up. "The spirits are aware of our presence," I said, clambering off my cousin and neglecting to mention the obvious: that everything in a half-mile radius was now aware of our presence. I grabbed my right toes and pulled them up toward my shin. My foot muscle relaxed, and I breathed a sigh of relief. "And now that we're aware of them, they should be easy to get rid of."

"Really?" asked Paula.

"You need to vacate by tomorrow morning," I instructed her. "We require thirty-six hours to make your house unin- habitable to all ghosts and spirits. You can return Monday evening to a beautiful California Craftsman that is yours and yours alone." I extended a hand and pulled Norbert to his feet. "Please remit the remainder of your payment online to Umbra Investigations."

AFTER PAULA HAD POURED herself another glass of booze and toddled back to bed, we headed for my GTO. Norbert plopped into the passenger seat and chucked our fake ghost-hunting equipment onto the seat behind us. "That was wild," he said.

"That was crap," I answered.

"Maybe."

I gave him a look. "You do know none of it was real, right?"

"Skeptic," said Norbert. It was what he *always* said. It drove me nuts.

"Paula's got bats in her belfry." I fired up the engine and pulled out onto the road.

"That's not very nice."

"I mean it," I said. "Actual bats."

"What?"

"Remember when I went up to the attic to measure the 'EMFs'?" I made air quotes with one set of fingers.

"Yeah . . ."

"Bat poo everywhere."

"The correct term for it is guano," my cousin said.

"Whatever. I'll have an exterminator come out tomorrow while she's gone."

"Then what about the lights?"

My cousin might be brilliant with technology; he might be an awesome (fake) paranormal investigator's assistant; he might be one of the only three family members I can stand to be around; but he doesn't know when to stop asking questions.

"Did you see any lights turn on? No. That's because Paula is a drunk. She forgets to turn them off when she's staggering down the hallway to her bed every night, and then she's surprised when she wakes up to pee and the lights are on. It's not ghosts. It's alcoholism."

Norbert sighed. "Sad."

"Stupid," I clarified.

LUCKILY, THE LOS ANGELES freeways tend to be pretty empty at midnight, so the drive back to the Valley was quick. Thirty-five minutes later, I was rolling down Norbert's quiet street.

"You want a ride on Monday?" I asked him.

He looked surprised. "Really? You'll drive me?"

I shrugged. "What, did you want to be dropped off by Mommy on your first day of high school?"

Norbert shook his head so hard that his brown ringlets danced. "No," he said. "It's just really nice of you."

I pulled up in front of his darkened house and turned to look at him. It wasn't something we ever discussed, but I had to assume that when Norbert had moved to California he hadn't been happy about it. He had been in the dead center of middle school at the time, hardly when you want to get yanked away from your friends and hauled across the country. It wasn't Norbert's fault that his cousin's family had melted down and his own family had ridden to the rescue.

"Sometimes I'm nice," I told him.

Norbert snorted. "Yeah, but I'm the only one who knows it."

I scooped up his alarm key chain from where it had fallen onto the seat and tossed it at him. "Be ready when I honk. I just scored a big case that starts on Monday."

"Really?" His eyes went round and happy. "Big like were-wolves and vampires and ghosts?"

Norbert kills me.

"No. Big like piles of cash."

"What's it about?" he asked.

"Same as always," I said. "Someone who believes in a bunch of crap that isn't true."

I was baiting him. Sometimes he's an intuitive old soul who puts up with my edges and walls. Other times, he's a little kid, fascinated by imaginary things that go bump in the night. Norbert opened the door and slid out into the darkness. Sure enough, he hesitated next to my car for a moment. His voice floated back through the open window. "Every myth has to start somewhere. Every legend carries a touch of truth."

Norbert *knew* I was a fraud—just the way my dad taught me to be—and yet he still wouldn't listen to logic.

"People have always been afraid of the dark," he continued. "Don't you think there's a reason for that? If this many believe—"

I couldn't take it anymore. "Do you know how many people used to believe the world was flat?"

"Oh, you still buy into that 'round' theory?" He dipped his head to grin at me.

"I'm out," I said, jerking the gear into reverse.

"Bye, Jillian."

I watched his dark shape trot away, grateful that Aggie and Edmund were already asleep in their world of matching dishes and mall-bought clothing. I didn't judge my aunt and uncle for their normal life. In fact I adored them for it, but the downside was that they were always so focused on trying to feed me or to set me up with "nice boys" or to convince me I needed highlights in my superstraight, superblack hair. I knew their attempts at parenting me were an expression of love. But every bowl of soup, every introduction to a tennis pro or youth group leader or Trader Joe's bag boy—it was all a big, horrible reminder that I didn't have parents of my own.

Not anymore.

NORBERT AND COMPANY LIVE nearby, so it was only a few minutes before I was picking my way through the overgrown backyard behind the house where I grew up. Even though I still showered there, it hadn't been *home* in over a year. It was a museum, enshrining the trappings of a family that had ceased to exist.

fake
JILLIAN CADE ∧ PARANORMAL INVESTIGATOR   9

My true home was over the garage: a tiny apartment at the top of splintered wooden steps.

That being said, when you have a father who lives a lie and taught you to do the same, no place feels like home. The ground beneath your feet is unstable. Every day is an earthquake day.

My dad traffics in bullshit. He built a tarnished empire out of selling snake oil to the stupid, the superstitious, and the desperate. Yet he still has legions of loyal followers who attended his lectures on the occult or signed up for Skype-chats about the paranormal. They continue to buy the books he sells through Echo Press, a crummy little publishing company run by his sketchy friend, Ernie.

Early on, Dad positioned himself as an expert on all things paranormal, and people bought into it, so he put himself on the front lines.

Umbra Investigations: my family curse and my financial salvation.

Dad had been carrying out these "investigations" since before I was born. When I was little, he occasionally brought me along while he drove around LA, taking photos of purportedly haunted locations for his website. Sometimes he let me press the camera buttons; other times, he posed me beside abandoned houses or gravestones. My mom didn't like it, but Dad said it was part of my heritage. Now he was out gallivanting around the world in search of yet more fraudulent magical artifacts to hawk to his followers.

His followers, I might add, who were more important than his only child.

The largest part of me looked down on everyone involved—on him for being such a blatant shyster and on the people who so eagerly paid money to lap up his fictions—but there was a sliver of me that understood those he duped. After all, if your greatest wish is to find something to believe in, something bigger than yourself, something that allows the world to make sense . . . well, maybe you're open to craziness. Maybe you cling to it.

And that's why I had clients.

My father was going to come home someday, and when he did, he'd still need a job to pay the bills. To my knowledge, there was no backup plan. This was the only career path I'd ever known my father to have, so I figured I'd better keep the PI doors open. Besides, it wasn't like he always remembered to send a weekly allowance. Someone had to scrape up the cash for food, not to mention the down payment on my car.

Sure, if I hadn't taken up the fake ghost-hunting mantle, Norbert and his parents would've happily taken me in. But then I would've had to fling myself under a bus. Besides, by now I'd figured out how to manage this whole (fake) paranormal investigator thing.

It wasn't all that hard.

Since most people don't entrust their weighty paranormal cases to seventeen-year-old chicks, I operate undercover. Potential clients have to submit an application on the Umbra website. I give them a quote, and they make the payment online. After the money comes in, I give the client a set of passwords to use when meeting "the operative" (me) at a convenient location (convenient for me). We prove our identities to each other with the passwords.

That's my favorite part because I usually assign them words that are obscure or weird. It's always funny seeing them try to work the first one into a random sentence to someone who might be an undercover paranormal agent with a youthful appearance, or who might just be a teenaged girl loitering in a 7-Eleven parking lot.

Occasionally I have Norbert run backup, in case the client turns out to be a crazed perv. It happened once. Norbert nearly ran the guy over with my car, which actually said more about my cousin's driving than about his outrage or powers of intimidation. But sometimes I leave Norbert out of a case altogether. Like the one I had starting that Monday, on the first day of school. It wasn't one I could chance letting Norbert screw up.

It was a first of its kind. It was a *real* case . . . or at least my new client thought it was.

I FLOPPED ONTO THE futon and opened my laptop to review Monday's information. I would be meeting this new client—site name: "HelpMeDude"—at lunchtime on my school's campus, where he would alert me to his identity with the four random passwords I'd given him: *blanket, asparagus, skateboard,* and *Guam.*

I scanned HelpMeDude's answers on the online form. I had asked for big bucks because it wasn't the usual love potion or ghost extermination.

Type of case:

| missing person |

Name of missing person:

| Todd Harmon |

Age of missing person:

| 21 |

How many days missing:

| 1 |

Suspected paranormal activity:

| cursing |

Suspected paranormal activity bit aside, it seemed like the cops should have been on it. Not me.

Of course, the cops didn't need the money like I did.

Umbra. It means the darkest part of a shadow. Exactly where I live.

TWO

Monday morning, I shambled barefooted and bathrobed from my apartment to the house. Not even seven o'clock and it was already warm. That's how it goes when you live in the San Fernando Valley. What we gain in relative proximity to the ocean we pay for in degrees Fahrenheit. Once I reached the plastic garden gnome gracing the back porch, I unscrewed its head and fished the key out of its hollow neck. I know other people stash their extra key in a fake rock, but that's not my life.

WHEN I WAS A kid, our house hadn't seemed creepy. Back then I'd thought it was cool. We had clocks with hieroglyphics instead of numbers. Statues of animals that didn't exist in real life. Candles and crystals and incense cones. Dusty books competing for shelf space with rolled up maps and glass jars of sparkling liquids.

I'd thought my life was magical.

Of course, that was before I knew there was no magic and that anyone could go broke buying up other people's discarded junk on eBay. It was before I understood that all I had to do to get my own sparkling liquid was bring a fake ID down to the local liquor store. It was before Mom's mind started slipping away. It was before the crying, and the staring, and the rambling about things that made no sense— *"The bridge! The bridge!"* Before Dad's desperation to heal her made him crazy too. That was life until she died and Dad fled the continent in search of epic adventures, fake treasures, and even more suckers to con. Life until I became the lone member of the Cade nuclear family.

TWENTY MINUTES LATER, I was back over the garage, tugging on a pair of tight, ripped jeans and shoving my feet into the Harley-Davidson boots I scored at a yard sale last year. I threw on a black tank top with the word EVIL scrawled across the front in scarlet thread. Then I smudged a thick line of black around my eyes, smeared crimson over my lips, and mussed a handful of product into my hair until the strands fell like cracks around my face.

Summers are long. Students forget state capitals and quadratic equations and how to diagram a sentence. I wanted to make sure everyone remembered exactly who I was: The Girl Who Shall Not Be Fucked With.

As I headed out, I paused to turn off the light before remembering I didn't have to. It was already off because so was the power. My fault. I had forgotten to pay the bill.

AS I APPROACHED NORBERT'S house, I wondered how long Aunt Aggie and Uncle Edmund would continue to let me live *fake* (above "CADE")

alone. Dad had talked them into it when he left last year. Since they lived so close, they could watch out for me without *hovering*. But of course no one thought I'd fly solo for this long. A couple weeks on your own is one thing. Living as an adult for an entire year when you're only a sophomore—and now a junior—is a different story.

I pulled into Norbert's driveway and gave the horn a quick tap. Sure enough, he scampered outside accompanied by his parents. Of course they wanted to see their kid off to his first day of high school. It's what any responsible parent would want.

"Angel love!" chirped Aunt Aggie. It had probably been unrealistic to think she would ignore me slumped behind the wheel of my own GTO.

I cranked the window down and gave her the best smile I could. "Hi." It sounded weak, even to me.

Aunt Aggie didn't care. Her arms swooped through the open window, and she hugged me in a way that no badass should ever be hugged. I couldn't return the favor because my elbows were pinned to my sides, so mostly I just fluttered my fingers against the sleeves of her cotton housedress.

"I can't believe you're in eleventh grade!" she trilled.

"Mmph," I managed from where my face was pressed into her shoulder.

Aunt Aggie finally released me. I averted my eyes from the red smudge my mouth had left on her dress. No need to blot my lips then.

As Norbert slid in beside me, Uncle Edmund dropped

a paper sack onto my lap. "Muenster and sweet pickle on white with mustard," he said.

"You didn't have to—" I started to say, but he waved off my protest.

"A brain needs nourishment. You kids have a great day at school."

"Thanks." I jammed my car into reverse and backed out of the driveway.

"Bye!" called Norbert.

"I love you!" sang out Aunt Aggie, waving.

Uncle Edmund gave a military salute. "So say we all!"

In my rearview mirror, I watched him sling an arm over Aggie's shoulders. They stood there, both of them beaming, as we drove off.

We were a block away when my cell buzzed from the backseat.

"I got it," said Norbert. He performed some very interesting calisthenics as he twisted and stretched to get my backpack without unbuckling. Finally, he sat back up straight, holding my phone. "Text from your dad."

"Delete," I told him.

"He wants you to send him some records," said Norbert. "They're in—"

"Did he happen to mention anything else? Maybe tell me to have a nice day at school?" I took a corner with a little extra aggression.

"No," said Norbert. Then *his* cell phone buzzed.

"Let me guess."

Norbert looked at his phone and nodded. "Your dad."

"Delete."

"You should call him."

"You should mind your own business," I said. "Besides, I don't have the time."

"The new case?"

"I got this one," I told him, holding firm. This case was actually sort of real, after all. It was no place for my wide-eyed cousin.

"Oh." Norbert looked crestfallen. "But what about school?"

"I told the client to meet me on campus at lunch. He's only dropping off a file. It'll be an easy grab."

"All right," said Norbert. "But if you need help later, let me know, okay?"

"Deal," I said, not meaning it.

AS IT TURNED OUT, I didn't even have time to worry about Norbert. Once we arrived, he went on his merry little way without so much as a backward glance. Good for him. My hope was that no one would mess with him once they realized he was my cousin.

The rise of my infamy had coincided with my mother's spectacular spiral downward. The first person to make a public comment about her had also been the last. It had been Mario Amello, captain of the football team. He had a good foot and at least a hundred pounds on me, yet he had gone home with a bloody lip, three sprained fingers, and a pair of seriously bruised testicles. I came away with a one-week suspension and a reputation for violence that prevented any hope of a future social life.

The upside: fewer distractions. The downside: a very specific kind of loneliness.

After I got my class schedule, I went searching for my locker. I trudged up two flights of stairs, past hordes of other students who were all exchanging hugs and waves and big dumb OMGs about their stupid summers. I caught pieces of conversations as they floated by me. Apparently, most of my classmates had toured colleges or gone to the beach or been, like, totally bored. No one else had fake-exterminated fake ghosts in fake haunted houses. Go figure.

I found my locker near the biology lab. Awesome: a year of smelling like formaldehyde. I dropped my backpack on the floor so I could dig the combination out of my jeans. Except the combination wasn't in my right pocket. Or the left one. Or either of the back ones. Really? This? Already?

I was reaching down for my backpack—maybe I had shoved it in there after all—when I heard a voice from behind me.

"Six, thirty-nine, seventeen."

I spun around. Standing in unacceptable violation of my personal space was a tall guy with messy blond hair, green eyes, and bright white teeth. Also, an inappropriate number of angles and muscles. For no apparent reason, my heart paused for a second, recovered, and kept beating . . . a little too quickly.

That was new.

The guy wore what looked like a military jacket covered with musician buttons and metal pins. He smiled down at me, brandishing a slip of paper between two of his fingers. My locker combination.

"It fell out of your pocket."

"You shouldn't be looking at my pockets," I snapped, snatching the paper from him.

He was obviously brand new, gathering from the fact that he was (a) still smiling at me, (b) hot, but (c) not yet face-suctioned to Corabelle LaCaze or Angel Ortega. Those girls had game for miles, whereas I still didn't even know the location of the stadium.

"I like pockets," he said.

I could see what was going on. He was trying to assert his dominant place in the social hierarchy by messing with me. Or by flirting with me. Or by messing with me _while_ flirting with me. Regardless, it was just what I didn't need: a hot, deviant pickpocket on my ass (literally). I turned and concentrated on opening the lock. And trying to ignore him. But after two failed attempts at getting the combination right, I had to admit to myself that I couldn't focus. He leaned against the adjoining locker, watching me . . . and apparently enjoying himself.

It made no sense whatsoever. It was high school, for crap's sake. There had to be a cheerleader or two around that he could gawk at.

"Do you mind?" I asked.

"Not at all."

I finally succeeded in yanking open the padlock. I slid the shackle out of the locker handle. "Ask around about me," I said, avoiding his eyes. "If you're looking for a new school romance, you're barking up the wrong girl. I'm not the chick with a tough exterior concealing a wounded, golden heart, the one who's aching for the right guy to notice her so he can crack her shell and sweep them both into the sunset. I might look like that girl, but I'm not her."

"Then which girl are you?"

"The one who wants to be left alone." Even as I said it, there was that teeny-tiny part of me that knew it wasn't true, but I forged ahead anyway. "I'm Jillian Cade, and chatting with me is not going to improve anything about your life, especially your social standing."

My monologue did nothing in the way of discouraging him. In fact, it appeared to have the exact opposite effect. His green eyes widened. He straightened and suddenly got all formal, jutting out a hand toward my own. He was even closer now, close enough for me to get a whiff of minty toothpaste and boy shampoo.

"I'm Sky Ramsey, and if your father's name is Lewis, then I beg to differ. Chatting with you *has*, in fact, improved my life. Significantly."

Ah. There it was. He wasn't talking to *me*. He was talking to the daughter of Lewis Cade.

I didn't answer.

"You are the single pro next to a very long list of cons about moving here," he added, dropping his hand when it was clear I wasn't about to shake it.

There was no reason to be disappointed. Despite the fact that this guy—I mean Sky—was much prettier than the usual flock of Lewis Cade fanboys, that's exactly what he was. Another brainwashed lemming looking to fling himself over the cliff of my father's lies. God forbid a normal boy be into me, just once.

"You are a fan of fiction," I informed him, "not a fan of me."

Sky raised an eyebrow. "Fiction?"

I was great at promoting my father's paranormal baloney when operating undercover, but I drew the line at real life. Fake Me ran my father's fraudulent cases. Real Me called it like it was.

"Poorly written fiction," I clarified.

"One man's trash is another man's treasure," said Sky. "I've read everything your father has written—poorly or not—and the truth is that I would love to meet him."

"You're too late. He's away on business."

"I'm not going anywhere."

"It might be permanent." My voice hardened. "And even if he was here, I've got better things to do than arrange his playdates."

Sky laughed. "Funny," he said, which startled me. No one at school ever thought I was funny. Then again, I wasn't exactly the class clown. He reached out to touch my arm. "Look, I didn't ask to move to Van Nuys. Your name is the one familiar thing around here. I'm happy to meet you. That's all."

He gave my arm a gentle squeeze, and before I could think of anything to say in return, he sauntered away down the hall. I stared after him, wondering what had just happened. I turned back to my locker. I was about to toss my Muenster and pickle sandwich inside it when I realized it wasn't empty. Leaning against the interior wall was a brown envelope.

What the hell?

I pulled out the envelope, ripped open the top edge, and upended it. A torn scrap of paper—maybe the size of my palm—fluttered out. I lifted it and scanned the printed text.

"What. The. Hell."

This time I said it out loud. The thing I was holding made no sense. It had no reason to exist.

It was a piece of newspaper.

An obituary.

My obituary.

THREE

JILLIAN ALICE CADE of Var
Nuys, California, died on Sunday
The daughter of Lewis Cade an
his late wife Gwendolyn, the
high school junior was a private
investigator of the paranormal. In
addition to her father, Ms. Cade
: survived by her sister, Ro:

And that's where the rest was ripped away.

Was it supposed to be a joke? Faking a piece of newspaper seemed like a lot of work. It didn't *feel* like a joke. It
felt like a real piece of newsprint.

It also felt like a threat.

BETWEEN THE OBITUARY, THE upcoming client appointment, the
run-in with my father's fanboy, and several calls from
my father himself (ignored), I had a hard time paying

attention in either Geometry or Chemistry. Luckily, it was all first-day BS: speeches about expectations for the year. When copies of grading policies and test schedules were handed to me, I shoved them into my backpack. Everything else, I tuned out. I needed to talk to Norbert.

Obeying my strongly worded text message, he met me near the history classrooms before third period.

"I don't understand the question," he said before I could speak.

"It's simple. Of the guys I've dated—"

"You don't date," said Norbert.

"I've been on dates." It sounded defensive, even to me. "There was that guy the summer before last. The one in Santa Monica."

"That wasn't a date," Norbert told me. "Getting drunk and making out under the pier is not a date."

"He bought me a Slurpee."

"Oh yeah? Then what was his name?"

"Dusty." I said it with more conviction than I felt.

"I thought it was Rusty."

"Whatever. My mother had just died. I was coping." I snapped my fingers, remembering. "And last year, I went to the movies with Michael Wilkins."

"Doesn't his mom play mah-jongg with my mom?"

"Who cares? Do either of those guys seem certifiable to you?"

Norbert considered. "I don't think so. And by the way, my first day of high school is going great. Thanks for asking."

I scowled and handed him the scrap of paper.

He looked it over and blinked a few times. "Whoa. Unnerving."

"Now do you get my questions?"

"How do they know about your PI work? Nobody knows about that."

"I hardly think that's the weirdest thing on that paper."

Norbert glanced up at me. "Who is this sister Rose? Do I have another cousin?"

"No!" I said it a little too loudly. A passing senior in a football jersey turned to look, and I glared in his direction. He sped up. I lowered my voice. "No sisters, no brothers. You're the closest thing I have to a sibling."

Norbert's eyes went all dopey and grateful like an anime fairy's. "You think of me as a brother?"

"Don't let it go to your head—and no hugging," I added hastily as he took a step toward me. He must have gotten that instinct from his mother.

"Going from cousin to brother is a clear indication of leveling up," he said.

"You're still *actually* my cousin, and I'm *actually* going to punch you if you don't focus. My potential demise is on the horizon."

Norbert returned his gaze to the scrap of newspaper. "Okay, so someone is trying to upset your equilibrium."

"In other words, it's a death threat. Don't sugarcoat. Do you think I pissed off a former client or something?"

"If so, they're giving you a big head start. Look." He pointed at the date on the newspaper. "Six months until your potential demise."

He was right. March 11. At least I had a running start.

"Go," I told him. "You don't want to be late to class."

"Copy that." I felt a flash of guilt as he took off down the hallway. I probably *should* check on him, I thought. Given some of the dickheads prowling the halls, it would be shocking if he made it through the day without getting beaten up.

AS IT TURNED OUT, I didn't need to worry about Norbert at all.

The next time I saw him was at lunchtime in the cafeteria. He was sitting at a table with what I assumed were two other freshmen: a boy wearing a WHAT THE FRAK? shirt and a girl who was demonstrating what appeared to be some Hogwarts-style wand work.

My relief over Norbert's acceptance into a clique—however dorky—was tinged with just a touch of envy. His first day of high school and he'd already found his tribe. Me: I had always been slow to bond, slow to trust, and once things had started going downhill at home, it was all over. The few acquaintances I'd made in the first half of my freshman year disappeared along with my ability to invite people to my house.

I waved to Norbert and headed back out, soda in hand—past the sundial and through the horde of front-lawn students who were tapping frantically away on their phones.

Even though everyone did it, we weren't technically supposed to text inside the school building. As a result, the lawn transcended cliques—tiny personal screens both include and exclude everyone—so I usually found a place to eat alone out there. But that day I'd made certain to be far from the mob. I threaded my way through it to a low-growing magnolia tree on the edge of campus. Beneath the tree was a bench, mostly hidden from view by a thick explosion of lilac shrubs. It was often empty, due to the abundance of birds pooping on it from the branches above.

This was where I had told HelpMeDude to meet me.

Unfortunately, as I saw when I arrived, it was also where senior Corabelle LaCaze had chosen to hang out.

Crap. Apparently bird poop doesn't affect hormones. But I should have figured. Everything that made the bench perfect for a covert fake detective meeting made it equally perfect for a covert make-out session. I didn't know who Corabelle was currently dating, but her tongue hadn't spent a lot of time in her own mouth last year. The girl was something of a rock star. If she'd had a way to bottle and sell her sex appeal and self-confidence, I would have happily bankrupted myself buying it. It wasn't just the way she looked. It was how she moved and spoke and breathed. She assumed the world already loved and wanted her, whereas I assumed exactly the opposite about myself.

In both cases, the world lived up to our expectations.

Corabelle was perched on one end of the bench, bright blond ponytail tilted back, big round boobs tilted forward. First day of school and—of course—already in the cheerleader outfit. She didn't look any more thrilled to see me than I was to see her. However, and to her credit, she greeted me with something that passed for politeness. "Hi."

"Hi." I dropped my backpack to the ground, plopping onto the other end of the bench. I glanced at my watch. Eight minutes.

First thing first: get rid of Corabelle. I decided to fight fornication with fornication. "I need this space," I told her. "I got a guy coming."

"Really?" Corabelle's tone of surprise was, frankly, a little offensive.

I frowned.

"Sorry." She didn't look sorry at all. "I've just never seen you with a guy."

I scanned the street. No cars were slowing down as they drove past the school. Yet. "Maybe I don't have guys the way you have guys, but I have guys."

"What is that supposed to mean?" Now *she* sounded offended. "The way I have guys?"

"Hi, guys."

It was a guy's voice. Actually, it was *Sky's* voice. He sat down between us on the bench.

Wonderful.

"Hello," Corabelle cooed.

Wonderful . . . and also irritating. I shrugged off any faint idea that Sky might have been interested in me, or that Corabelle *wouldn't* be interested in him. With his messy crop of dirty-blond hair and the way his face was all perfect and his body was all tall and lean, it made total sense that she'd jumped right on it. But seriously, school had started like four hours ago. It wasn't her taste that was so impressive. It was her speed.

Now I had seven minutes until my client showed up,

and I had to ditch two audience members instead of one. This was awful . . .

Or not, I suddenly realized.

Since Corabelle and Sky appeared to be meeting for some noontime nookie, maybe there was a way to get him to take her somewhere else. After all, she wasn't going to let him get to second base right in front of me. At least, I hoped not.

"Condoms," I blurted out.

Corabelle stared at me. "What?"

"She said condoms," Sky told her helpfully.

"They're giving them out in the cafeteria," I said. "It's part of the war against sexually transmitted diseases. You guys should go pick some up."

"What are you trying to say?" Corabelle asked.

"Only that you might want to take advantage of the free prophylactics being offered at our oh-so-progressive school."

"I'm on the pill," said Corabelle.

"But these are special condoms. Like, with colors and flavors." I was improvising now, which couldn't be good. Outside of that one embarrassing week in seventh-grade health class, I'd never come in contact with a condom in my life. "And shapes."

Sky and Corabelle exchanged glances. "Shapes?" he said.

Corabelle shrugged. "Hey, if you want to check out the condoms with shapes, go right ahead." She fixed me with a glare that was both icy and amused. "I'm comfortable right here."

"Me too," said Sky.

What did they want, a witness for their exchange of bodily fluids? They would not win this battle. They could get it on anywhere. I was staking my claim on this bench. I checked my watch again. Five minutes. Still no cars. I was debating faking a coronary, because maybe at least one of them would run for help, when Corabelle said something that changed my mind.

"You know what would make this bench even more comfortable?" She stared straight at Sky. "A nice thick blanket."

I froze.

Blanket? Did she say *blanket*?! The first of my four random passwords? It had to be a coincidence. It had to be merely a weird way of inviting Sky's lips onto her own. Surely—*surely*—my rich HelpMeDude client was not Corabelle LaCaze!

I looked at Sky. He was smiling at Corabelle. "If you don't mind getting bird poop on it," he said.

"Oh." Corabelle kept her gaze on Sky. She could have been disappointed about one of two things: either that Sky hadn't said the second password or that he hadn't lunged into her mouth. The latter seemed more likely.

There was only one thing to do. I leaned toward Corabelle, trying to ignore Sky between us. "I agree with you," I said.

Her giant blue eyes turned to me. "You do?"

"A blanket would be great out here. It could be used for a picnic."

"A picnic?" Corabelle also leaned closer.

"A fancy picnic," I said. "One with gourmet cheeses and spiced olives and baguettes."

fake

"Anything else?" Corabelle's eyes never wavered from mine.

"Champagne?" said Sky. We both ignored him.

"Vegetables," I said.

"Vegetables," Corabelle breathed.

We drew closer until we were practically in Sky's lap. He didn't seem to mind. "Green beans?" he asked.

"No," I said. "No green beans."

"Definitely no green beans," said Corabelle.

I stared straight at Corabelle, letting the word slide slowly from between my lips. "Asssssparagusssss."

Corabelle's eyes and mouth popped open super wide. "Only if you cooked it on a skateboard!" she shrieked.

Okay, now that was just stupid. Mine at least made sense.

"A skateboard in Guam," I concluded.

Corabelle leaped to her feet. "Holy shit! *You're* Umbra Investigations!"

And then she burst into tears.

FOUR

I leapt up, holding my hands out to shush Corabelle. The girl cried *loud*. "Let's go somewhere else," I urged in what I hoped was a soothing voice. I glanced at Sky. He already knew too much about my father. No need to share even more information about my secret life as a (fake) paranormal detective.

But Sky didn't seem to take the hint. He pulled a tissue out of his backpack and handed it to Corabelle.

"Don't leave on my behalf," he said. "Umbra is the bomb."

I whirled to him. "That's it. Get lost. Find some other girls to bother. This isn't your party."

But Sky only grinned at me, leaning back on the bench with his hands laced behind his head. "But it's the most interesting party in town."

I scowled. Fanboy of my dad or not, what kind of jerk sticks around where he's clearly unwanted? I opened my mouth to tell him what I thought, but Corabelle interrupted.

"It totally makes sense that you're Umbra," she gasped between sobs. "If anyone at this school was going to be a paranormal investigator—"

Fake, I added in my head.

"—it's you. You're so weird and dark and scary."

"Thanks," I told her. "Look, let's go where we can talk. *Alone*. I'll buy you a coffee and—"

"It's in Jillian's DNA," Sky interrupted. "Her father is basically a guru when it comes to the paranormal, so of course she's a genius with this stuff. You're in great hands."

I glared at him once more before focusing my gaze on Corabelle. It was time to try a different strategy: ignoring Sky completely. "What's with the HelpMeDude handle?" I asked her. "I thought you were a guy."

"I meant to type Help*My*Dude, but I hit the wrong key."

She blew her nose, and Sky fished out yet another tissue for her.

Ignoring wasn't working either. And something occurred to me. Sky was being helpful. Really helpful. *Too* helpful. In my limited understanding of cute boys, even the ones who are fanboys of Daddy Dearest, they don't go this far out of their way without a hidden agenda. Something was off about Sky Ramsey. Something that maybe I could have figured out if I had been a real detective.

"So you've got a case?" he asked Corabelle.

I wanted to kill him, but I let it go for a moment because I didn't want to scare Corabelle away. And because she was taking deep, calming yoga breaths beside me. She dabbed her eyes one last time. "My boyfriend is missing."

"You have a boyfriend?" Sky and I said together.

fake

Apparently I hadn't been the only one thinking Corabelle was tongue-gunning for Sky. It must have bummed him out to see his lunch-hour sexy time disappear, but at least now he might take off in search of someone who was more available.

"Todd Harmon, like I wrote," Corabelle said. "He's a junior at CSUN."

Of course he was.

All right, time to get Sky out of here. I made shooing motions. "Okay, you've seen enough. Go away. This is a confidential case."

"He can stay," said Corabelle. "I don't mind."

"I can stay," Sky echoed. "She doesn't mind."

"You *can't* stay because *I* mind," I informed them both.

Sky stared at me. "Interesting."

"It's not interesting and it's not your business. Goodbye."

"You know, the way you say 'confidential,' Jillian . . . it doesn't sound like you mean it." The smile he turned on me was slow. Deliberate. "It sounds like you're just making that up. It sounds like . . . *fiction.*"

The blood in my wrists went icy and sluggish. Sky wasn't just *off.* He was blackmailing me. He was using my own words from earlier against me—the ones I'd said when it hadn't occurred to me that he would ever be a witness to my fake detective work. But why *would* that have occurred to me? I began to feel panicky. Maybe he'd appointed himself to be the hero who exposed the lies of the Cade family. Maybe he wasn't a fanboy after all.

Maybe he was the opposite.

"There's no fiction here," I said, inwardly scrambling

for a way to defend myself if he outed me as a nonbeliever in the paranormal to Corabelle. "There's just me trying to do my job."

"All I'm saying is I would enjoy watching you do that job. After all, it's always amazing to see someone who is truly gifted in their . . . calling." The way he paused before the last word confirmed it: Sky was epically screwing with me, and if I wasn't careful, I was going to get epically screwed.

The only question was *why*.

"Please go." It came out more pitiful than I intended.

"As you wish," said Sky, standing up. "I want to help, but I'm pretty busy anyway. It turns out that I have some really interesting *facts* to publish on various social media outlets." He pulled out his phone and started swiping and tapping. "Mostly a global bulletin about Jillian Cade, the great paranormal investigator and the strongly held *beliefs* that compelled her to become involved with this business in the first place—"

"Fine!" I interrupted. "Stay, Sky. Please. Help if you want to help."

"Are you sure?" Sky awarded me another (unfortunately) brilliant smile.

"I'm sure." Inwardly, I wondered if it was possible to suffocate him with a wad of his own Corabelle-soiled tissues. It was clear: I had no choice in the matter. I was going to have to roll with this—at least temporarily. I turned back to Corabelle. "Saturday, on the application, you said Todd had been missing for a day." I unzipped my backpack and rustled around for a pen and notebook. "You still haven't heard from him?"

fake

"Nothing."

"So three days. Since Friday." I scribbled it down.

"Is that when you last saw him?" asked Sky.

"I got this," I told him with a glare. "If you want to help, just *listen*."

"No, that was Thursday night," Corabelle answered.

"Out of curiosity," I asked her, "why haven't you called the police?"

"Do you happen to know a cop who'd believe my boy-friend was cursed?"

And here we go.

This would usually be when I clicked into full-out bullshit mode. The problem was, this time I would have to do it in front of an audience member who was one hundred percent onto me, and whose motives I could only guess. I tapped my pen against the notebook.

"Hm," I said, my voice thoughtful to match the thoughtful face I was trying to make. "Cursed, you say."

I glanced over at Sky and saw that one of his eyebrows was raised.

"I know it sounds weird," said Corabelle.

"Not at all. Curses are Umbra's specialty. Tell me more."

"I mean, he's a twenty-one-year-old guy," said Corabelle. "Of course he's going to go out partying with his friends. I don't expect us to spend every waking minute together."

I could see where this was heading. Corabelle had hooked up with a college guy and couldn't take it when he blew her off. Way better for her ego to assume it was a curse than to accept what had probably actually lured him away: a hot coed with an interest in anatomy.

Now that I thought about it, this was going to be a piece of cake.

I'd find out who Todd was dating and then tell Corabelle I'd broken the curse. Yet in doing so, I'd say that I had learned the identity of Todd's soul mate. I would woefully share that it was not Corabelle, and I'd "prove" it by showing her photos or videos of Todd with his collegiate flavor of the month. Then, to assuage her grief, I'd throw in a free charm to attract a love of her own.

Since Corabelle had never had a problem getting male attention, she'd have another guy on top of her within minutes. Maybe it would even be Sky. I could play it off as a supernatural sign that he'd shown up right as Todd had bailed out. I could kill two birds with one stone and wash my hands of the whole stupid affair, many dollars richer. Not too bad, all things considered.

"What was the first sign that he'd been cursed?" I asked her.

"We were supposed to go out Wednesday night, but he canceled on me." I scribbled. Sky made a tsking sound. Corabelle kept going. "Todd had a headache, so instead we decided to meet for breakfast before he went to work the next day. At the restaurant on Thursday morning, he was all weird and distracted. And he smelled . . ." She paused and I waited. "He smelled like he'd been burnt."

My pen hovered over the notebook. "Burnt?"

Sky leaned forward on the bench, his smug expression gone. Now he seemed to be listening intently.

"I don't know how else to explain it," said Corabelle. "It

wasn't anything like barbecue smoke, and it wasn't exactly like cigarettes either. It was—"

"Hellfire."

That would be Sky who said the word. Sky, who had no business throwing himself into *my* business, who was now standing and pacing in front of the bench. "It sounds like hellfire," he said.

No, really. What did he *want?*

Corabelle nodded. "If that's a thing, that's how I'd describe it."

"Was it sulfuric?" Sky asked. "You know, like a lit match?"

I was getting fed up, fast. It wasn't enough that he was blackmailing me. Now he had to play Mr. Amateur Fake Detective too?

"That's not relevant to—" I began. And then I stopped. What if that *was* it? What if Sky wasn't playing annoying amateur detective but was, instead, the real (fake) thing? Another pretend pro trying to move in on my turf. It had never happened before, but there's a first time for everything. And it made sense, given all his interest in my father.

Or maybe I was just jumpy because someone had slipped an obituary into my locker.

Either way, I had to indulge him. At least in front of Corabelle. Once I had Sky alone, I'd be able to find out what he was up to.

"Yeah, sulfuric," Corabelle answered Sky. "And then, all the rest of the day, it was radio silence from Todd. No calls. No emails. Nothing. It wasn't like him. He always sends me texts from work, little things . . . you know, for my eyes only."

Barf, I thought.

"Nice," Sky said.

Corabelle smiled gratefully at Sky. "That's the thing. He even stopped playing Words With Friends. Right in the middle of our game. He never came back to it. It was awful."

Tragic.

"So we are still talking about Thursday," I said for clarification.

"Yes."

"One workday," I said, on the off chance I had somehow missed a key piece of information. "Literally eight hours where Todd didn't call you or text you or play turn-based word games with you."

"Right," said Corabelle.

"Did you see him Thursday night?" Sky cut in.

"Yes, but not for long. I went over to his apartment."

"Uninvited?" I asked.

She ignored the question, keeping her eyes on Sky. "His roommates were playing poker."

"He didn't join in?" asked Sky.

"No," said Corabelle. "He sat in the corner and watched them."

"Was it like he was in a trance?" said Sky.

Corabelle nodded, swallowing. "Exactly. His eyes were all red."

I bit my lip, forcing myself to stay quiet. I reminded myself of the facts: Corabelle was the one with the checkbook; Sky was the one with the goods on me; and I was the one with the fraudulent business practices.

"Were his lips dry?" Sky pressed. "Did his hands shake?"

"Yes!" Corabelle sat up straight and began nodding. "Both of those."

I cleared my throat loudly. Sky was hitting too close to the mark. Too close to *my* mark. Unless . . .

Another possibility crept into my mind.

I hopped to my feet and took a hard look at Sky. He was good-looking, tall, with some muscles but not in that too-much-time-at-the-gym way. Mature. Maybe older even. And he grilled Corabelle with assurance. The kind of assurance that didn't seem amateur at all.

What if Sky wasn't an amateur detective or a fake pro? What if he wasn't even a student? What if he was the real deal, as in, *real*—an actual young-looking cop stationed on school grounds to investigate me?

What if *I* was the mark here?

I wasn't one to pore over academic guidelines, but I was pretty sure that running a bogus paranormal-investigation business on campus was against school rules. And probably against legal ones too.

Shit.

"So Thursday night was the last time you laid eyes on Todd?" I asked Corabelle, determined to keep what little control I had over the situation.

"Yes," said Corabelle. "I told him I'd wait for him in his room, but he never came in. I finally fell asleep. When I woke up, he was gone. His roommate said he went camping."

That sounded suspicious. On the other hand, maybe Todd was one of those guys who had to tramp around in the woods and commune with nature when he was working something out . . . like how to dump his high-schooler girlfriend.

"I know it sounds crazy that I think it's a curse," said Corabelle, "but I read about it online."

There you go. Another belief that my clients have in common: if it's on the Internet, it must be true.

"I started with Google because I was trying to find articles about keeping a guy interested. I ended up on a website selling love spells." She paused. "I was curious, okay? Anyway, I found some site that was talking about love *curses*, when love gets reversed. It's like the opposite of a love spell. It's the only thing that makes sense. Some other girl saw him and wanted him for herself." Tears welled up in her eyes. "He's been gone for three days straight. I don't know if he's alive or . . ." She burst into tears again.

"Come here," said Sky.

He pulled her to her feet and right into his chest, hugging her close. I wasn't sure what to do, so I gave her an awkward pat on the shoulder.

Corabelle raised her head and looked up into his eyes. "Do I sound crazy? Maybe I should call the police."

Maybe she should, I thought. Maybe she didn't even need to pick up the phone. Maybe she was standing in the arms of the police right at that minute.

Still, I needed the money. Badly. My dad's house didn't even have electricity right then, for crying out loud. So unless I wanted to move in with Norbert's family, if there was a chance that Sky really was what he might have been pretending to be—Hot New Guy, Fan of Bullshittery, and Protector of Gorgeous Teenaged Rock Stars—then I needed to stay on task. I needed to seal the deal with Cora-belle, end this gruesome threesome, and handle Sky later.

In private.

Still, I felt a tiny, confusing pang as Sky-Who-Might-Destroy-Me soothed my client. He was good at soothing.

Finally, he pulled back and looked Corabelle in the face. "Now listen," he said. "The hellfire, could you smell it on Todd's clothing?"

"On everything," Corabelle answered in a little-girl voice. "In his hair and on his breath too." She reached mascara-smeared fingers into her purse and pulled out a folded piece of paper. "Here. I wrote down all the things I could think of. His work information and cell phone number, everything."

Instead of handing the paper to me, she handed it to *him*.

"Don't worry," Sky said. "We'll find out who cursed your boyfriend. And then we'll *find* your boyfriend." From behind Corabelle, he flashed me the sweetest of smiles.

Maddening.

FIVE

The bell rang immediately after Corabelle signed my nondisclosure agreement, which I desperately hoped she understood—*she couldn't tell a soul;* I repeated that part out loud—and handed me an envelope full of cash. At least she gave *that* to me. I assured her I would be in touch.

Only then did Sky trot away. Convenient timing.

I would have chased him down to force an explanation out of him, but our school doesn't give us much time to get to class. I raced to my locker and then into my literature class right as the teacher was about to close the door. I flung myself into the only empty seat: front and center, which happened to be right next to Sky Ramsey.

"Really? You had to take Greek Mythology too?"

He shrugged. "The other options were Short Stories of the Depression Era or Dystopian Literature. This sounded more uplifting."

I turned to face the whiteboard. I thought about punching him. There was a tap on my shoulder and I whirled. "What?!" I snapped.

But Sky's hands were folded on his desk, his gaze fixed straight ahead. I caught movement out of the corner of my eye and turned back to see a familiar girl named Lauren. Or maybe Laurel. We had been in Algebra together last year. She was in the seat behind me, one hand clutched against her chest, her eyes huge and terrified. "I'm sorry," she whispered. "I just . . . uh . . . your pen fell."

I followed her trembling finger to where my pen lay on the floor.

"Thanks," I said to Lauren-or-Laurel, not sure why she was *that* scared of me. Maybe she had been in the cafeteria that day in ninth grade to witness the kicking of Mario's ass, or maybe it was just because she's one of those girls who seems to be afraid all the time. Now that I thought about it, I couldn't remember a single time she'd raised her hand in class. If a teacher called on her, she went all shaky and could barely get the answer out.

"It's my favorite pen," I lied as a peace offering.

Lauren-or-Laurel mustered a grateful smile. "It's an awesome pen," she breathed.

I wasn't sure what to say to that, so I picked up my "awesome" pen (run-of-the-mill Bic, institutional blue). As I uncapped it, I had a depressing thought: maybe every kid at this school was messed up in some way. Maybe they all needed healing. Or maybe, like me, they all had secret criminal lives.

Probably not.

More likely: maybe everything was exactly as it appeared. Lauren-or-Laurel was a quivery basket case, Sky was a

fake

hot-but-pushy student or cop, and I was the only screwed-up freak among us.

AS USUAL, I SPACED out during class—alternating between obsessing about the obituary and wondering if Sky Ramsey was a narc—while Mr. Lowe welcomed us and droned on about his expectations. Really, these teachers needed to get some new material.

When the bell finally rang, I shoved everything into my backpack as quickly as I could, but somehow Sky was able to scoot out the door ahead of me. I charged after him, but he was too fast, too nimble. By the time I reached the hall, he had already vanished into the crush of students.

I didn't spot him again until the day was over. Turns out his locker was down the hall from mine. He was shoving books inside when I marched up. He slammed the door and turned to me, a picture of confidence: all white smile and tanned skin and green eyes.

"Hi, Jillian!"

The place was mostly cleared out, so I had nothing to lose. "Look, you and I both know there's no such thing as a curse, so what the hell are you doing?"

His smile didn't waver. "Some people would say I'm being helpful."

"Some other people would say you should butt out."

"Well, those people would be rude, wouldn't they?" Sky didn't seem bothered at all. In fact, as he leaned against his locker, he seemed amused.

No other guy at school had ever looked at me like that, like he was seeing past my reputation to *me*. No one pushed back. No one even engaged with me. No one cared enough.

So why did Sky?

I wasn't sure exactly what the rules were, but I thought there was a thing about how police officers had to identify themselves if specifically asked. I jutted a finger into Sky's face.

"Are you a cop?" He hesitated and I took a step closer. "I know my rights," I lied. "You have to tell me if you're a cop."

"Fine." Sky took a deep breath. He finally lost his smile. "I am a cop."

Quick waves of emotion crashed over me.

First, victory.

Second, horror.

Third, anger.

He shook his head. "Okay, you got me on the cop thing. Don't tell anyone, and we can work together to find Todd Harmon. Deal?"

Fourth: I was familiar with the smell of bullshit, and the odor had just become overwhelming. Sky stuck out a hand for me to shake. I looked down at it for a second. This was way, way too easy.

I raised my eyes. "Let me see it."

He grinned. "Wow, a girl who knows what she wants."

"Not *that* it!" I whapped him in the chest. "It! *It* . . . your badge. Hand it over."

"I left it at home."

Uh-huh.

"Cops don't leave their badges at home."

fake

He blinked. "We prefer the term 'law enforcement officers.'"

"I prefer the term 'big fat liar.' If you're a cop, prove it. Read me my rights."

"Fine. You have the right to remain silent. Anything you say can be used against you in a court of law."

"And?"

"And that's it."

Yep. I definitely wasn't the only one pretending here. I pulled out my phone and opened a search engine. "There's more to the Miranda rights than that."

"No there's not."

I touch-typed on my tiny screen. "There's something else. Something about lawyers or courtrooms . . ."

"Court of law! I said 'court of law'!" Sky tried to grab my phone, but I skittered backward, holding it out of his reach. "Come on, stop it."

"Not until you tell me the truth."

"All right. I'm not really a cop." Again, he looked amused, which only annoyed me more. "Did you honestly believe I was?"

I crossed my arms in front of my body, assessing him. Maybe if I gave him a little truth, he'd give me a little in return.

"Look, my father's not here, so you can't impress him or get his autograph or whatever. I *have* to help Corabelle because I need to keep Umbra alive and going until he gets back. Why do you want in on it?" I gazed up at him and (lame) fluttered my lashes, trying to channel Corabelle mesmerizing a guy. "Please, just tell me. Why do you care?"

Sky turned away. He raked a hand through his hair, making it even messier than usual. After a moment, he turned back. "Okay, here's the deal. I think Todd has been selling drugs at CSUN. The hellfire smell is from cooking meth."

"That's a lot to get from twenty minutes with Corabelle."

"Maybe." Sky wasn't smiling anymore. "But I'm willing to guess that a lot of your cases involve people who drink or use drugs."

I thought of Whack Job Paula from Saturday night. I kept silent.

"I'm not judging you or your dad or your profession. You know I think it's awesome. It's just that you might be on the wrong track here. Maybe Todd Harmon got made by the cops and dumped his stash. Maybe he's on the brink of getting whacked by somebody who wants his money back."

"Maybe you have an overactive imagination." Even as I said it, I remembered a recent news story about a drug house in Northridge. It was certainly more plausible than "hellfire" and a cursing.

"I'm telling you this . . . because the same thing happened to my friend in Albuquerque." The last part tumbled out of Sky's mouth in a rush. His eyes fell to the floor. "He was my good friend. My *best* friend. He was only trying to pay for his sister's education. His parents were gone, so he was all she had. Then he got diagnosed with cancer. He thought he didn't have long to live, so he started cooking. He got mixed up with the wrong dealers and ended up dead." Sky looked off into the distance. "When he died, it was the worst thing that ever happened to me."

My fists clenched at my sides. I wanted to believe Sky, because what kind of jackass argues with a person in mourning? Yet my very short history with this particular person was defined pretty much by its very long list of lies. I had no way of trusting him. That being said, I realized I could probably make him *think* I did.

I placed a gentle hand on his arm. "I'm so sorry."

Sky swallowed. "Thank you. I don't want to see it happen to anyone else, you know? I think this could all be fate. I think we were *meant* to come together so we could save Todd Harmon." He tilted his head to look down at me, and as I looked back, I knew I was lingering a little too long on those green eyes. Something about Sky Ramsey made me want to believe, to say yes to anything he asked. It wasn't just that he was new, that he was good-looking, that he'd latched on to me . . . Well, maybe it *was* all those things. Still, I wanted to tell him that it could work. We could figure this out together. We could be a *team*.

But I don't let guys screw me, and I don't let guys save me. And at that moment, I wasn't sure which one Sky Ramsey was trying to do.

SIX

There is a beautiful lake in Echo Park. Surrounded by palm trees, it's dotted with ducklings and lotus flowers and paddle boats. Three graceful plumes of water shoot up from a center fountain. A view of the Los Angeles skyline is visible from its shores. It is serene. Lush. Gorgeous.

The lake went by in a blue-green blur.

I was driving to a *different* part of Echo Park, the part the real estate pages and websites don't mention. The one with litter-strewn streets, chain-link fences, and graffiti-sprayed walls; home to my destination, a grubby strip mall. I slid out the driver's side door and walked past a Chinese diner, an insurance company, and a Laundromat. I imagine that Echo Press doesn't have the kind of neighbors most publishing houses do.

Tiny and dark, the office was papered with the company's work: election brochures, business cards, neighborhood weeklies . . . and of course, framed covers of my father's books. Behind a high wooden counter sat the owner, Ernie Stuart.

It had been at least a couple years since I'd last seen him. In that time, his ever-present mullet had started to slide down the sides of his head, leaving his skull gleaming through the strands of hair left atop it.

Ernie peered at me for a second before he made the connection. "Jilly!" He rose to his feet, arms spread wide, and embraced me over the counter. "Look at you, all grown up. How are you doing, sweetie?"

"Fabulous," I told him.

Lies come easy to a professional liar.

"You know, I've been hoping you'd pop by and come see me," he said. "I would've gone to your mom's funeral—"

"But there wasn't one. How's it going here?"

"Eh," he said. "Slow. You need something for your dad?"

I shook my head. "I was wondering if you could take a look at something . . . for me. On the DL."

"The DL?"

"Down low," I said.

"You kids."

I pulled open the envelope and dropped the obituary—*my* obituary—on the counter. I watched Ernie's eyes skate back and forth over the words before lifting to meet my gaze. "Joke or a threat?"

"I'm trying to figure that out," I said. "Is it a real newspaper?"

Ernie slid a fingertip around the edge of the scrap, then nodded. "Feels like litho. Cold, probably. Or heatset. Maybe web-fed."

I blinked at him. "Uh . . ."

"Sorry. What I mean is, any press could've done it."

"So there's no way to find out who?"

"Leave it here. I'll call around."

"Thanks. I owe you one."

He made a copy of the obituary for me. I thanked him again and headed for the door. I was almost there when he spoke up.

"Funny you should come by today. I got an email from your dad."

I stopped in my tracks and turned around, trying to make my voice sound casual. "Yeah?"

"He'll be home soon," said Ernie. "But I guess you already knew that."

"Sure." I hoped my tone sounded appropriately optimistic. "Can't wait." I ducked out. The last thing I wanted to do was celebrate the purported return of my father, back from his yearlong self-imposed sabbatical from life . . . from me.

Besides, there was no way it would actually happen. My dad was an even more seasoned professional liar than I was.

I was so busy zipping the copy of the obituary into my backpack that I didn't notice Sky Ramsey until I was almost on top of him. He was leaning against my car, legs crossed at the ankles and arms crossed over his chest. I stopped short. That white smile floated over his face.

"What are you getting printed?" he asked.

"None of your business." I reached for the door handle, but he blocked it with his body.

"Funeral programs for Todd Harmon? You're going to need them if you don't get on top of our case."

Our case? Unbelievable. It was *my* case, period. He'd simply blackmailed his way into it. Anger simmered below the surface of my skin as my eyes traveled over him, this guy with the too-bright teeth and the too-intense gaze who was acting way too interested in me.

"You stalked me from school."

He nodded. "I wouldn't use the word 'stalked,' but yeah. And it wasn't easy. You drive too fast."

My jaw clenched. "Before that, before the driving-fast part, did you happen to notice what I was up to?"

"You were sitting in your car in the school parking lot, doing something really important on your phone. That reminds me, what level of Candy Crush are you on?"

I returned his smirk. "I wasn't playing Candy Crush. I was doing research. In fact, I had a breakthrough. I made a really important discovery about the Todd Harmon case. *My* case."

"Awesome! What did you find out?" He sounded genuinely excited. As if he could convince me, as if I could believe anything about him was genuine at all, other than a genuine talent for lying. Maybe he was a professional like my dad and me.

Time to find out.

"I thought it was really terrible, about the meth and your friend in Albuquerque. What did you say his name was again?"

"My friend? Bryan."

I almost laughed. That was the clincher. "Right. A real tragedy."

Sky nodded. "Super tragic."

"Everyone must have been so sad."

"There was a big funeral."

"Flowers?"

Sky looked at me funny. "What?"

"Flowers. Were there lots of flowers?"

"Sure. Tons. They filled the whole church. Roses mostly. White ones. Some red—"

"Stop it!" The words exploded out of me.

"Stop what?"

"I didn't research Todd Harmon! I researched your meth-cooking friend, except that you don't *have* a meth-cooking friend! You told me the plot of *Breaking Bad.* Bryan Cranston? The actor who played the lead? How stupid do you think I am?"

Sky's smile faltered. "I don't know what you're talking about."

"I'm talking about you being a liar! Todd Harmon is not a drug-dealing would-be victim of gang murder."

"Fine." His lips pressed into a tight line. "Then what do you think happened to him?"

"Nothing!" I yelled. "He's just a cheater! He's a guy with a heat-seeking missile aimed at a campus full of coeds. It's sad, but it's classic, and because I need the money, I have to take this stupid case and figure out who he's seeing so I can somehow break it to Corabelle!"

"I hesitate to use the word 'blowing' right after your missile metaphor—"

"Then don't!"

"But you're blowing it," he finished. His tone had changed; he wasn't mocking or playful anymore. "Todd isn't cheating on Corabelle. At least not in any traditional sense of the word."

"That's it." My hand plunged into my pocket and emerged with my cell phone. "You really *are* a stalker. I'm calling the police."

"Too bad. You really *are* beautiful," Sky said, imitating my voice as he whipped out his own cell. "But you are also a fraud and a bullshit artist. So go ahead and call the police. While you're telling them all about me, I will be calling Corabelle to let her know that you don't believe in the curse and you don't believe in her."

I searched my brain for a comeback. "You don't have her number."

"I got it in fifth period," he said. "Government and Economics."

Of course. My eyes turned to slits. We stood there, staring at each other, holding our phones out like old-west gunfighters in a standoff. Finally, I slid my phone back into my pocket.

"What do you want?" I demanded. "I mean, really. From *me*."

"To get to know you," he said.

The perfect answer. I nodded. Not because I believed him, but because I *wanted* to believe him. I wanted that perfect answer because Sky Ramsey was challenging in a way that I had never been challenged before. He wasn't trying to save me; he acted like I could actually use some help. Like I was funny instead of scary. Like I was the person I wanted to be instead of the person I truly was.

"Then why are you blackmailing me?" I asked.

fake

"So you'll take it seriously."

"You or the case?"

"Both."

I crossed my arms. It wasn't only because it's what you do when you think something is absurd. It was also because Sky's body suddenly seemed much too close to mine. I needed a barrier between us. I needed a barrier because . . .

Otherwise being that close to him might start to feel tolerable.

Or, worse, good.

"Listen," Sky continued. "It could have happened that my parents never met. Dad could have turned a corner a second too late, Mom might have chosen a different restaurant, and I never would have existed. Same thing with your parents, but fate aligned exactly the right way at exactly the right time. Like this morning. I just happened to be at your locker. You just happened to drop your combination." He bent closer. "I'm telling you, it was fate. We met so we could get to know each other. So we could save Todd Harmon together."

Right. Of course. Someone who believed in the paranormal would also believe in fate: two things I knew didn't exist. And as much as I would have loved to fairy-tale my way into a hot high school romance, there was one very important *fact* (to use one of Sky's terms against him for once): he *was* blackmailing me.

"It's not fate," I told him. "It's a public education. We both have mythology class, so I would have met you there anyway. You're still a creep. An insane, stalking, blackmailing creep."

"You don't believe that."

His voice was so quiet that I could barely hear him. I wanted to jerk my gaze away from his but I couldn't. He leaned down and I found myself stretching up, meeting him halfway, our heads almost touching in the thick, still air of the parking lot. "I think you trust me enough to solve this case together."

And then he took a step forward. Got closer, right *there*, close enough for me to see the flecks of gold in his green eyes. He didn't touch me, but he might as well have. Something radiated between us, something I had definitely *not* felt with Dusty-or-Rusty. Something that made my skin go hot and my breath go fast. Sky dipped his head, bringing his mouth to my ear. "I think we can do lots of things together."

I didn't really plan to jerk my knee up into his groin. It just sort of happened.

The energy between us vanished, his mouth exploded in a bunch of colorful words, and he dropped to the concrete, rolling to the curb in a fetal position. I yanked open the GTO's door and got inside. As I fired up the engine and backed out of my spot, I caught a glimpse of him in my rearview mirror, struggling to his feet.

For some reason, as I pulled into traffic and turned the steering wheel in the direction of the Valley, I didn't think about how dangerous this guy might be to my reputation or to the fraudulent Cade family business, to my *future*. No, only one piece of information burned its way to the front of my brain. It wasn't about Corabelle LaCaze. It wasn't about Todd Harmon. It wasn't even about my obituary. It was about one thing Sky had said and the way that he'd said it. The way it was different from the threats and the lies.

It was this: Sky Ramsey thought I was beautiful.

SEVEN

As anyone who's ever suffered through a late afternoon drive from Echo Park to Northridge knows, traffic sucks. I used the car time to blast the radio, hoping random pop music would erase Sky from my memory. It was nearly five o'clock by the time I reached the small medical clinic not far from CSUN campus. Apparently Todd was pre-med (nicely done, Corabelle—well, except for the cheating thing) and had been helping out in the office over the summer as a way to gain experience.

I had to hand it to him: the guy seemed industrious, both in his career and his sex life.

As I turned off the engine, Norbert called.

"Jillian," he said, not even bothering with a hello, "Uncle Lewis has left six messages on my phone. Please, for my sanity, call him back."

"What does he want now?"

"He needs your mom's birth certificate," said Norbert. "He says it's in a red box inside the living room trunk. You can scan both sides of it and email it to him."

I groaned. "Did he happen to mention why?"

"I don't know, but just do it, please. I don't want any more messages. I don't want any more texts. I'm afraid he's going to start cyberstalking me."

"Fine," I said. "When I get home."

"I'll let him know."

"Thanks," I said, not meaning it, and hung up. I yanked the lever underneath my seat and shoved myself as far back as I could go. In a bag stashed in the backseat, I found a black pencil skirt and a demure white blouse. Getting into them while still in the car may not have been my most graceful work, but I got the job done. I buttoned the blouse over my T-shirt and slipped my feet into black heels (with little bows over the toes, no less). After twisting my hair back away from my face and slicking on some pale pink lipstick, I was satisfied.

Once I swung out of my car, I took a moment to try to straighten everything out. After tucking my phone into a glossy black handbag I'd found at the Salvation Army, I grabbed a clipboard from the backseat and closed the door.

Then I stepped directly onto Sky's foot.

"Ow!" He winced, shaking his foot. "Is there any part of my body you *don't* want to injure?"

I almost smiled. I should have expected him to follow me. Maybe I *had* expected it. "Off the top of my head, I can't think of one. Besides, how else can I convince you to leave me alone?"

Sky gave me the once-over. "How about you tell me why you're dressed like a secretary from the fifties?"

"I'm a pharmaceutical representative," I said before

turning and sailing away in a graceful blaze of self-righteous indignation.

At least, that was my intention. In reality, the stupid high heel on my stupid left foot caught in a crack on the stupid pavement and I nearly fell.

Sky caught me by the shoulders and held me up.

"See?" he said. "I'm not a creep. I'm nice."

I kicked my heel free of the crack and jerked away from him. "See? I am *not* nice."

Sky nodded toward the clinic's cracked sign: BARON & PEEBLER OBSTETRICS. "Is that where you're going?"

I didn't even bother to answer. There was no point in either telling the truth *or* lying.

He checked his watch. "It's five minutes until five. It sure would suck if the clinic closed before you had a chance to go in. Then you'd have to wait until tomorrow afternoon to gather any more intel on Todd."

"Is that your way of inviting yourself in with me?"

"Yes, if you promise not to step on my foot or kick me in my balls again."

"I can't make that promise," I said with a glance at the clinic. My options were running out. I could stand around and argue with Sky, or I could accept that I was stuck with him. On the plus side, maybe there was something to that old adage about keeping your friends (of which I had none) close and your enemies closer. If I let Sky tag along, he would eventually slip up, and I'd find out his real deal . . . or I'd prove that he *was* nothing more than a hot fanboy of my father's fiction. One who also appeared, inexplicably, to have a thing for me.

Of course, I knew the latter was improbable. Or more accurately, impossible.

"Fine," I said. This time, I managed to turn with something approximating dignity. He followed right behind me as I strutted up the sidewalk. Two little bells chime-chimed when I opened the door.

We stepped into the waiting room, and Sky looked around, taking in the violet-flowered wallpaper and wicker furniture and Anne Geddes calendar. "Quaint," he said.

"Barf," I said.

I arrived at the counter right as a ruddy-cheeked nurse bustled out of a back room. She looked between the two of us. "We don't have any more openings today."

Sky let out a disappointed sigh. I pinched the back of his arm—hard.

"We're not patients." I raised my clipboard. "I'm a PharmaHeal rep. Is Todd Harmon here?"

The nurse snorted and turned to her computer monitor. "Todd didn't come in today."

Well, that would have been too easy.

"Hmm." I tapped my clipboard. "Maybe you can help me. We had a computer glitch this week, and all our sheets are a mess. Do you know if one of my colleagues came by on Friday?"

"No idea," said the nurse. "Todd normally is our first point of contact for sales, but he didn't show up on Friday. Thursday either. College kids."

"Thank you for your time." I turned to leave.

"Wait a minute," Sky said, staying put. "Would you mind checking to see if PharmaHeal left samples?"

The nurse didn't look up. "I'm really busy."

"Please." Sky cleared his throat. When she finally lifted her head, he got all eyesy and teethy at her. "You would be saving me a lot of trouble with this spreadsheet."

The nurse blushed a little. Actually blushed.

I was reminded that having very good looks and being a very good liar is a very dangerous combination.

"Well, okay. Give me a second." She scurried away into the back.

Unbelievable.

Sky leaned over the counter and started flipping through the scheduling book.

"What are you doing?" I said. "Stop that!"

"Wednesday," he said, which made no sense whatsoever. He ran his finger down the page, then grabbed a Sharpie out of the cup of pens on the desk and scribbled something on the inside of his arm.

The first thing that popped into my head came out as a stage whisper: "That's permanent ink!"

"I'll exfoliate," he whispered, dropping the book back on the desk.

The nurse returned an instant later. "I don't see any PharmaHeal boxes."

Sky's fingers enclosed my upper arm. "Thanks. That's a huge help." The nurse fluttered her fingers at him as he pulled me toward the exit.

Once outside the building with the door safely shut behind us, I yanked my arm away from his grasp. "Stop touching me!"

Sky gave me a look that can only be described as *knowing.* Correction: *obnoxiously* knowing.

I scowled. "What?"

"Someday I am going to remind you of this time, of this very moment when you told me not to touch you." He leaned close to me. "And you are going to take back those words."

"In your dreams," I said.

The obnoxiously knowing look broadened into a grin. "Exactly."

Something inside of me snapped. "I can't take it anymore. The stalking and the smiling and the—"

"The what?"

"The arrogance. I can't stand the arrogance."

"It's not arrogance. It's awareness of our connection."

"Dial it back," I told him. "If you think you found something—a *real* something—let's have it. Spit it out."

Sky sighed. "Okay, but you have to promise to give me the benefit of the doubt. It's going to sound crazy."

"Crazier than a cable TV show starring Bryan Cranston?"

He hesitated, looking at me. "Todd Harmon was taken by a succubus."

"Maybe you misheard me," I said. "Tell me the truth. I'm waiting."

"A succubus," he repeated.

"Like I said, waiting. Because it sounded like you said a succubus."

"Right. It's a female demon who loves sex."

I nodded. "Sounds like Corabelle. *She* is a female demon who loves sex."

But Sky had stopped grinning. In fact, his face had lost any trace of humor. Even his gold-flecked eyes had darkened. "Todd is showing every sign."

fake

"Of another lay," I said. "Maybe of some party drugs. Even your bullshit *Breaking Bad* lie made more sense. How's that for irony?"

"I'm telling you, it's succubus addiction," Sky said. "That's why he was gone at night and couldn't focus during the day. Addicts can think of nothing but the succubus who's infected them. Nothing else can fulfill them."

Okay, so Sky was messing with me. I decided to play along, because maybe, at long last, this was a way to glimpse who he really was. "Okay, enlighten me. How do you get a succubus to stop screwing your guy?"

"Easy," said Sky. "Kill her."

"Excuse me?" I glanced around in case a passerby had heard his plan for paranormal murder.

"You know, make her dead."

"I got that. I just didn't—"

"Direct sunlight burns them. Like vampires."

My hands flung themselves into the air. "That's it. I'm out of here!" I marched toward my car, fuming. Just my luck that the first guy I'd been attracted to in . . . well, maybe in forever . . . was *this* guy. And I still wasn't entirely sure that *I* wasn't the one he wanted to make dead.

"Wait! Jillian, listen." Sky caught up to me, rattling off information. "On Thursday, Todd smelled like hellfire, and then he didn't make it to work. That means he had to have first contact before that, on Wednesday. We know he was at work, and the schedule book showed only one new patient that day. Nine o'clock. Jillian, *look*." He grabbed my shoulder and spun me around, then yanked up his sleeve to show me the words scribbled in thick black on his arm. It was a name: *Diane Bedloe*. "There's your succubus."

I blinked up at him. "You're telling me the truth right now. As in, that's actually what you think happened. A female demon sauntered in and kidnapped a gynecologist's intern."

"Of course not," said Sky. "Todd followed the succubus of his own accord."

"And why, exactly, would Todd do that?"

"Because she kissed him. One taste. That's all it takes."

"Okay, let me make sure I'm following." I started to dig through my bag for my keys. "Wednesday, a succubus named Diane Bedloe masquerades as a new patient and kisses Todd Harmon. Thursday, he has breakfast with Corabelle but then tragically stops sexting her. Corabelle sees him Thursday night. He refuses to give her his sweet collegiate man-love." I snap the bag shut. "Then he takes off Friday morning to follow the succubus."

Sky nodded. He'd been nodding the whole time, in fact. "Correct."

"Insane."

"Call it what you will, but do you have a better lead?"

Yes, actually I did. "No, I don't," I said out loud.

"Then help me track down Diane Bedloe," said Sky. "Help me find Todd Harmon. We can do this together. We can be a team."

My heart was sinking. It wasn't that Sky wanted to screw me; he wanted to screw *with* me. That had to be it, right? Because the only other option was that he really truly believed this stuff, and that *couldn't* be it. Sure, he was a pathological liar, but by all appearances, he wasn't *stupid*. And yet a tiny part of me came back to that damn word he'd used before: *fate*. I didn't believe in it. It was coincidence that he'd just said out loud the exact things I'd been thinking when I hadn't been thinking straight. That we could do this together. That we could be a team . . .

"Jillian, look at me." It was hard not to, being that he was right there in my face. "Yes, I lied to you about the meth thing—"

"And about the cop thing."

"Right, that too. But I'm not lying to you now, I swear. There are other things, things in this world that are beyond what most people think of as true . . ."

God, now he sounded like Norbert.

"Things that defy logic."

Yep, definitely Norbert talking.

"Things that are bigger than we are," he said. "Scarier. Darker. Jillian, please. Trust me."

I had never looked into a boy's eyes like this, not this close and not when he was staring back with this much emotion. Now I was doing it for the second time in one day. It didn't make any sense, and I didn't trust things that didn't make sense.

Also, I didn't trust people. Any people.

Especially this person.

"Why should I listen to you?"

"Because I can be a lot more than the guy who lies." He sounded almost pleading. "Or the new cute guy at school—"

"You're not that cute," I lied in return.

"Fine. Then because I can help you. If we save Todd Harmon, I can prove there's more to the world than what most people see."

"Why?" It had to be asked. "Why now, and why this, and why *me?*" He opened his mouth but I interrupted. "And don't say 'fate.'"

"Because I am not those guys. I am a very ordinary dude with a very ordinary life." Sky reached out and wrapped his hands around my upper arms. "But you, Jillian. You are extraordinary, and your life is extraordinary, and you don't even realize it. Just like your father, I believe in the darker, hidden parts of our world."

My father.

"And Jillian." He pulled me closer. "I believe in you."

As I stared up at him, I wanted to sink into Sky's version of me. I wanted to be that special girl he claimed I was, but I couldn't. I wasn't extraordinary. I was just weird. And sad. And lonely.

And most important: a fraud, like he'd said before. Like my father, whom Sky couldn't see as the fraud *he* was too.

I pulled away, taking a big step backward. "No. None of this is real."

"Jillian."

"Goodbye," I said.

Then I jumped into my car and headed west on Nordhoff Street to break into Todd Harmon's place.

EIGHT

Todd and his roommates lived in a sedate complex off Nordhoff and Darby. The break-in was absurdly easy. The spare key was exactly where Corabelle had said it would be: stashed under the GOT BEER? doormat. Honestly, I had expected something a little better from a pre-med student.

I knocked first. When no one answered, I let myself in. The apartment looked exactly like a place where three twenty-year-old dudes lived together. Old pizza boxes. Recycling bins overflowing with Bud Light cans. A San Diego Chargers jersey thumbtacked to the wall.

I skirted an IKEA table with mismatched chairs and tiptoed down the hallway. There were four doors: three bedrooms and a bathroom.

I ruled out the first bedroom because of the pink sticker over the doorknob that said, "Property of Meredith" in curlicue handwriting. *Poor Meredith's boyfriend.* I poked my head into the second bedroom—hockey sticks leaning against the unmade bed, a giant stuffed panda, an open *Playboy* magazine—and then into the third.

Bingo.

Right there on the nightstand was a framed photo of Corabelle. I picked it up. She was standing on a dirt path surrounded by trees. Patches of sunlight dappled her face, which was surprisingly devoid of her usual makeup. She was wearing a too-big CSUN shirt over muddy jeans. The shot had caught her midlaugh, her head turned slightly away from the camera, one hand pushing back her blond hair. She looked happy. Happier than I'd ever seen her at school.

Okay, so as of Friday morning, Todd was still waking up to a picture of Corabelle. That was something. I checked out the rest of the room. Basic double bed with off-white sheets and a tan comforter, unmade. Mainstream rock posters and a map of the world. A desk piled high with textbooks.

I opened Todd's closet and shoved through a dozen Oxford shirts in various colors. Sandwiched between a periwinkle and a salmon pinstripe was a patch of clothing that obviously belonged to Corabelle: a little black dress (emphasis on "little"), a red nightie, one pair of designer jeans, and two tank tops sharing a hanger. It was unfathomable. Corabelle—who was only a year older than me—kept personal things at her boyfriend's apartment. I couldn't imagine wanting to do that. I couldn't imagine someone wanting me to.

I was about to close the door when I caught a gleam of metal in the back corner. I pushed aside a half dozen pairs of khakis for a better view. It was a hook jutting from a small canvas bag. The bag clanked when I lifted it to look inside. More hooks and some clips. I dropped it on the floor and shoved the rest of the hanging clothing over to one side so I could see what was crammed in the back of Todd's closet—an orange, mesh, two-person tent.

Camping, my ass.

BACK IN MY CAR outside the apartment complex, I found I'd gotten another text from my father, two from Norbert, and one from a number I didn't recognize:

havent solved case yet. you?

Sky! How had he gotten my number? But the moment I sent the question, I knew what he would say:

Corabelle.

He followed this up with:

duh.

I turned on my car to head for home . . . and then I killed the engine. And sat there, pondering. Maybe there was something—granted, a very tiny kernel of some-thing—to Sky's theory. Our theories (mine and Sky's) had more in common than I'd originally thought. It was very probable that Todd was cheating on Corabelle with a girl. Sky believed that Todd was cheating on Corabelle with a succubus. When framed that way, our two theories weren't *that* dissimilar. If you took the crazy out of the equation, that is. Point being: maybe Sky and I *could* work together.

If Todd was indeed too much of a wuss to confess to Corabelle that he was with some chick, why *not* tell her it was a succubus? It fell in line with the lies—I mean, "mythology"—on Umbra's website and would probably pave the way to Corabelle accepting a "love charm" of her own as a partial solution. I could claim that the spell of a succubus is unbreakable, maybe even dig up some "evidence" to support this, and she would just have to move on with her life. Sky would go along with it because he would believe that the other girl really *was* a succubus. It was a win-win.

I pulled out my phone again and sent Sky a text message:

Can you meet me in 20 minutes?

He answered almost immediately:

where?

I sent him details and turned the key in my ignition.

SKY WAS ALREADY THERE when I arrived at the benches on the south end of Lake Balboa. As I plopped down beside him, two big white ducks in the water changed course and headed toward us. They didn't come on land but paddled right by the concrete edge, eyeing us hopefully. I hadn't brought any bread along, but I wasn't surprised to see them. I'd pretty much chosen this spot for the same reason I'd chosen the bench at school: there was a lot of bird poop around, in this case, duck poop; the benches tended to be unoccupied.

Sky swiveled so that his knee grazed my leg. "Did you find something out?" he asked. "Something succubus related?"

"Not exactly."

"A clue about where Todd might be?"

"More like a clue about where he's *not*. He's definitely not camping."

Sky frowned. "Then why are we here? You don't buy the

succubus theory, and you've been trying to get rid of me all day. Why the sudden change of heart? What do you want?"

I moved back a little. "Look, I don't have to believe in the existence of succubi to know something weird is going on with Todd Harmon. Also, although it pains me to say it, I acknowledge that you have a desire to help. And although you may say 'succubus' and I may say 'sorority girl,' at the end of the day, we're both trying to find the last person to lay eyes on Todd."

His green eyes sparkled. "So you want to work together after all?"

I held a finger up in front of his face. "Under one condition." I gave him a stern look. "If we are going to do that, I have to trust you. I have to know *why* you want to help. I have to know that you are being honest with me. So prove it."

"Prove what?"

"That you really believe in this succubus stuff. That you're not just messing with me. Go on. Tell me what you know—or think you know."

Sky looked at me as if *I* were the crazy one. "It's all from your dad. I was being serious when I told you that, Jillian."

My shoulders sagged. "Right. You're an expert on the famous Dr. Cade."

"I stumbled across a lecture on YouTube, and then I couldn't stop watching him. His bit on Zoroastrian eschatology was spot-on. His interpretation of the Vendidad was amazing. Once I heard what he had to say, I wanted to find out more. I wanted to know everything."

I nodded, hating that Sky bought into Dad's lies and yet also feeling relieved. If Sky had done this much homework, it was harder to believe that this was all one big practical joke with me as the punch line. Of course, it didn't explain why he seemed so interested in me.

"I also get why you're not into this stuff," he added. "There's so much bullshit out there."

"A lot of it perpetrated by my own family," I reminded him. "My dad included, Sky. You know that, right?"

"Right. Your father capitalized on superstition, and now you're doing the same thing."

"Only to keep Umbra afloat," I shot back.

"I'm not judging," said Sky. "Sometimes we all do things because the end justifies the means, but here's my point: not everything paranormal *is* bullshit. Not everything supernatural is false. Some of it is real; some of it is true. Your father would agree with me."

"But that's where you're wrong," I told him. "My father is a con artist. He doesn't buy any of it. The only thing he believes in is the utter stupidity of the people who swallow that paranormal crap."

Sky shook his head. "It's like Santa Claus. Your dad knows there's no jolly man in a red suit sneaking into kids' houses at night to give them presents. But he *also* knows that the story of Saint Nicholas came from somewhere, that it was based on something real. That's what's happening here. Most of Umbra's cases are pure fiction, but somewhere back behind the superstition and made-up nonsense, there's truth. Your father sees that truth."

I frowned. "You've never even met my father."

"I feel like I know him."

"That's ridiculous. *I* don't even know him." I clamped my mouth shut. Too much info to give a guy I'd only met that morning.

"I'm telling you, I've seen everything he's ever posted online. I've read every thesis and article out there. I would have signed up for one of his classes when I got into town, but . . ."

"But you couldn't," I finished. "He's not here."

"Right. He's not here." Sky gave me a gentle smile. "But you are, and I wanted to meet Dr. Cade's only daughter."

Unless he has another daughter named Rose. Remind me to tell you about that *sometime, Sky.*

"That's why I was at your locker. I was hoping to find you. By coincidence, you dropped your combination. Except that it *wasn't* a coincidence. It was fate."

I stared out over the waters of the man-made lake. In the spring, all the cherry trees surrounding it would burst into magnificent pink blossoms, and the whole place would look like a fairy tale. But at an hour before sunset in late August, it was only a regular old park hidden away in the middle of a very large city. The same way Sky was just a regular guy. No—worse. He was a believer in my father, which made him a sucker. It made me think less of him. It made him less attractive.

And maybe that was a good thing.

I turned back to him. "Okay."

"Okay?"

"Okay." I stuck out my hand. "You can tag along."

He smiled and shook it. "In that case, I've got news. Diane Bedloe isn't a succubus after all."

I had to smile back. "You think?"

"Yeah. Norbert did a search for me."

"Norbert?!"

"Yeah, Norbert. You know, your cousin?"

I glared at him, suddenly seething. "My cousin is off-limits. You *don't* talk to him behind my back—"

"Relax," Sky cut in. "He *wanted* to help. He came up with two Diane Bedloes within Los Angeles city limits. I tracked down the first one. Preschool teacher in Los Feliz. Not a succubus job."

I forced myself to calm down. I could very easily imagine *why* Norbert would be eager to help Sky—an older kid, relaxed and self-assured and handsome (i.e., everything Norbert was not)—especially since I'd shut him out of the case. "And just what is a succubus job?" I asked.

"One you can do at night or in shadows. When I was mapping the preschool online, I realized something. There are palm trees around the playground, but they don't give a lot of shade. That particular Diane Bedloe must spend a lot of time in direct sunlight, and—"

"Sunlight kills succubi."

"Exactly," he said. "Which means that the Diane Bedloe who was a new patient at Todd's workplace couldn't be a succubus."

I nodded. "Because she came in during the day."

"Right. And it's not like I didn't think of that in the first place, but Diane's appointment was at nine in the morning. You know how the marine layer always settles over the Valley

fake

on summer mornings? I figured she was still protected by the cloud cover, except that then I went back and checked Wednesday's weather. Remember how it was really hot last week? The marine layer burnt off early. There's no way a succubus would have been out in the daytime. She would have fried for sure."

Clearly there was no use being upset that he'd gotten to Norbert; they were meant for each other. I took a deep breath. "All right, so we're crossing Diane Bedloe off the list of potential succubi." I tried to sound like I meant it.

Sky squinted at me. "You don't mean it."

I couldn't win with this guy.

"You're right," I said. "I don't. But since I am temporarily allowing you to assist me on the case, I'm going to play nicely. At least, I'll try."

"There *is* a succubus loose in Los Angeles. That I know for sure."

"And if you're wrong?" I asked him.

He considered. "If I'm wrong, I'll leave you alone. Norbert too. Even when your dad comes back. Your whole family. Completely, utterly, totally. Happy?"

Oddly enough, I wasn't, but I nodded anyway. "Beyond happy."

Sky leaned closer, lowering his voice. "However, if I'm right . . ."

I gazed back at him, once again too close to those green eyes. The seconds ticked past. *Not attractive, not attractive, not attractive.*

"What? What if you're right?" I demanded.

Sky grinned and tilted away from me. "I'll let you know."

I stood up, relieved. "Then I'll get busy holding my breath. See you tomorrow."

He didn't follow me. Instead he called to me from the bench as I walked away. "Bye, partner."

I knew he was still smiling.

NINE

By the time I pulled into my driveway, the sun had almost disappeared. The sky was darkening, along with my mood. I was more tired, hungry, and confused than I'd been in a while—a considerable feat, considering I'd been fending for myself the past year. I was holding way too many questions in my brain and way too many emotions in my . . . wherever emotions live: anger at my father, fear about the obituary and what it meant, confusion about Sky, frustration with Corabelle's case. Not to mention curiosity about who this "Rose" person could be.

Funny: as usual, an Umbra case was the only thing in my life over which I had some small measure of control.

I decided to focus on it.

Todd seemed like a reasonably together guy—job, school, apartment, eyes on the future. So if he lied about going camping to his friends and ditched work, something really might be off with him. Something more than just a girl. I made an internal note to ask Corabelle if she knew about any history of mental illness in his family. Tomorrow,

of course. Right now I needed a granola bar. Or a half
bag of stale chips, or an apple, or a bowl of cereal without
milk. Those were the options awaiting me . . .

Shit. I was almost to my garage stairs when I remembered what I'd promised Norbert: Dad's stupid red box.

I let myself into the back door of my father's house. It
was really dark, so I slid my hand up the interior wall to
the light switch. I flipped it up . . . and nothing happened.
Oh yeah, the electricity. The other thing I'd forgotten:
pay the final past-due notice. One of the big reasons I
needed Corabelle's case in the first place.

With both arms blindly stretched out before me, I shuf-
fled ahead until the floor under my high heels changed
from wood to linoleum: the kitchen. Reaching out to
the left, my fingers closed on the handle of a drawer and
pulled it open. After a second of groping around the cluttered interior, I found what I was looking for—a box of
emergency candles and a book of matches.

After all, we did live in earthquake country.

I lit a candle and used its flickering light to find one
of my mother's delicate china saucers. Drops of wax fell
on the porcelain until there was enough to secure the
candle in place. Holding my makeshift torch, I pushed
open the slatted saloon doors separating the kitchen
from the living room. They creaked when they swung
shut behind me. A cobweb drifted over my face. Yet more
reminders that everyone who used to live here was now
somewhere else.

I made my way to the couch and placed the saucer on
the side table. The trunk doubled as a coffee table, so I

had to clear the knickknacks off the top before I could open it.

A soft rapping startled me. It took me a second to make the connection that someone was knocking on the front door. I closed the trunk and hopped up. Even before I yanked the door open, I knew who would be there. Apparently my day was going to both start and end with this guy. Sky held a white paper bag against his body, almost like he was cradling a baby, and shouldered past me, ignoring my huff of indignation. "We didn't discuss our plan for tomorrow."

"Are you kidding me?" I was past being polite. "Enough already! You have my phone number. Use it!"

Sky didn't seem perturbed by my outburst. "I did use it."

"No you didn't."

"Yes I did."

"No you . . ." My voice trailed off. I stopped and ran my hands down the front of my jeans, then the back. My phone wasn't in any of those pockets. I stormed back to the sofa where I had dropped my backpack and ripped it open. I was starting to rifle through it when Sky spoke again.

"Looking for this?" I turned to see him holding up my phone. "You left it on the bench."

A long moment passed—one in which I could have screamed or kicked him again or called the police. But I saw his smile in the uncertain light, and more importantly, I caught a whiff of whatever was in that white paper bag. He held it up before me. "Hungry?"

I laughed. I couldn't help myself. If he wouldn't leave

me alone, I might as well get a free meal out of it. I gestured toward the couch. "Have a seat."

Sky's head turned to the right and then to the left. "I appreciate romance as much as the next guy, but I can barely see you."

One of his hands moved toward the panel of switches by the front door, and I panicked.

"No!" I shouted, leaping forward and grabbing his arm.

Too late. His fingers brushed over the panel, and of course, nothing happened. He looked down at me, but I was frozen, still grasping his arm, humiliated. I had gotten used to the dimness in the room. I had forgotten. Of all people in the world, why did it have to be Sky Ramsey who knew the electricity had been turned off?

His hand floated back to where mine was clenched on his arm, and he gently disengaged my fingers. He was still looking at me, puzzled. Or worse, pitying. Paralyzed with shame, I could only stare back. We stood like that for the barest moment, and then I felt a pressure on my fingers—a squeeze—and he let go.

"You must have blown a fuse," he said and headed toward the couch.

I swallowed. "Yeah. Old houses."

"Old houses." I heard him pat the cushion beside him. "Come on."

I sat and waited while Sky pulled out burgers. He handed one to me. I lifted it to my mouth and took a bite. It was beyond delicious. I took several more bites.

He handed me a napkin, then set two Cokes on the trunk. When he shifted his weight, some of the knickknacks _fake_

on the cushion beside him clinked together. Sky picked one up from the pile and held it near the candle. It was a photo of . . .

"Dr. Cade," Sky said in a voice that was hushed and reverent.

I took another bite of burger, watching him.

"When will he be back from his leave of absence?" Sky asked me. "All the info online said that he left to . . ." He paused, looking at me. "To help your mom," he finished.

I didn't plan to snort, and yet I did.

"What?" he asked.

I didn't have to tell him the truth. I could have lied to him like I did to everyone else. I could have given him the party line: Dad was overseas when Mom suddenly got sick. She passed away before he could get home. It was tragic and unexpected. I could have said that, but I didn't have the energy to spit out another lie.

So instead, I set my half-eaten burger down. I reached over and plucked my father's picture from Sky's hands and tossed it on the other side of the couch—my side, out of his reach. Instead, I told him what had really happened.

"She took months to die," I said.

Sky set his burger down too. He stared at me.

"The doctors did tests until our insurance ran out, and she got sicker and sicker and then lost her mind. I had to lock her in her room so she couldn't run away. I almost failed out of ninth grade because I skipped school so many times, and my aunt and uncle moved back from North Carolina . . ."

I could feel something right behind my eyes. Hot.

Prickling. Unfamiliar. I turned away from Sky, toward the photo next to me.

"During all of it, Dad was gone," I went on. "He wasn't here when she got out and came to school and broke the cafeteria windows. He wasn't here when she wrote, 'Burn the bridge' a thousand times across the floor. He wasn't here when she . . ."

I paused. And swallowed. Hard.

". . . when she hurt herself."

I felt rather than saw Sky move closer to me.

"He was in Egypt." Every word was a struggle. "He was in Jordan and Greece and Algeria. He was everywhere else."

Sky's fingers covered my own.

"He wasn't here the night she stopped breathing," I said, yanking my hand away.

That's when the tears came.

Sky started moving toward me. "Jillian—"

"Get out," I said.

And he did.

TEN

I slammed my father's bullshit red box onto my bed. Except it wasn't even red. It was more like burnt orange. Old coral. Rotting peach.

Whatever.

I slung my handbag down by it. The latch popped open, and my cell phone skittered out onto the mattress. I grabbed it and checked the tiny screen. One missed call. I thumbed the screen as I plopped down next to the box. The message was from Ernie Stuart.

"Hey Jilly, hate to tell you, but I got nothing on your fake obituary. I'm thinking it's a joke. How many guys you juggling?"

Yeah, right.

"I bet one got pissed. I'll ask my buddy to run prints, but I think it's probably nothing. Take care of yourself, kiddo—"

My thumb pressed down.

"Message deleted," said a mechanical voice.

I dropped my phone onto the mattress and lifted the

box's lid. Might as well get this over with, for Norbert's sake—at least the night couldn't get any worse. I had a concrete job to do: find my dead mother's birth certificate. Easy. Depressing. Awful. Much like the rest of my life.

Inside was my father's usual mess of illegible handwritten papers and files and typed documents. I flipped through until I found a folder marked *birth certificate* and then tugged a paper from between the faded flaps. There was my mother's name—Gwendolyn Cade—right at the top. Perfect. I could give it to Norbert and let him deal with how to send it to my father. The last thing I wanted was to—

Hold on.

I drew the yellowed paper closer to my eyes. This birth certificate was the wrong one. It didn't list my mother as having *been* birthed. It showed that she had *given* birth.

To a baby.

A baby who wasn't me.

The certificate documented a live birth that had happened sixteen years ago. A live birth with a name.

Rosemary Cade.

If this was real, I had been fourteen months old at the time.

I scrambled to rip open my backpack and the envelope inside. The obituary copy fluttered out onto my bed. There it was, literally printed in black and white.

In addition to her father, Ms. Cade is survived by her sister, Rose—

And nothing more.

THE NEXT MORNING, AGGIE and Edmund only waved from the window as my cousin headed toward my car. I was certain they wouldn't give me any information about my potential sister—apparently the one thing my family does well is lie—but it would have been satisfying to make them squirm.

If they even knew about her, that is.

As I waved back, it seemed less likely they knew anything at all. My dad was the liar, not them. So instead of asking them about it, I took it out on Norbert. In my defense, I'd been planning to yell at him anyway.

"Now you're Sky's personal assistant?" I demanded as soon as he hopped into my car. "Who do you work for, anyway?"

Norbert scowled. "If anyone here should be mad, it's me," he shot back. "I'm your cousin. I get to do your grunt work."

"Yeah, so?"

"So how come you partner up with Sky and not me?"

"Sky Ramsey and I are not partners!"

"Oh, really?" said Norbert. "So he just *happens* to know you're Umbra Investigations. He just *happens* to have all the information on the Corabelle LaCaze case? He just *happens* to need a name run on a potential suspect?"

"He barged into my client interview. It was an accident!" I stepped on the gas and sped down the street.

Norbert made a noise through his nose.

"Look, he's obsessed with my dad," I said, gripping the steering wheel. "He was dying to be a part of Umbra. I didn't go to him. He came to me."

Norbert folded his arms and turned his body away from me. "Whatever. It's cool."

He was silent the rest of the way to school. When I parked, he reached for the door handle without a word. I needed to do something. It wasn't *his* fault that my life was a series of surprise disasters.

"Norbert!"

He didn't answer, but he froze in place.

"I need your help."

His hand still on the door, he turned and looked at me, his eyes softening. "You do?"

"I need everything you can find on Todd Harmon. Cell phone activity, driver's license, plates, parking tickets. Anything. I've never had a missing person case before, and . . ." I paused, but only because the next part was true, and truth is not exactly my specialty. "It's a big deal. I can't do it alone."

Norbert grinned. "I'm on it. You're welcome."

I FOUND CORABELLE IN the hallway before homeroom. She wasn't her usual manicured self. Her ponytail had slid halfway down her head, and some strands had escaped the rubber band to straggle around her face.

"Did you find Todd?" she asked the moment she saw me.

"Not yet." I pulled her into a corner so we could have some semblance of privacy. "But you're right. It's totally a curse."

She blinked rapidly. Her hand went to her mouth. "I knew it."

Sliding back into my Umbra mode was the easiest thing

in the world. Ignoring the twinge of guilt over lying about Todd Harmon—a real missing person—was more difficult. Giving a crap had never been part of the Umbra plan. I shook it off. "There's some dangerous magic at play here," I told Corabelle. "I don't know if you're aware, but Van Nuys is the warlock capital of the world."

"Really?" she breathed.

"Yeah, and I hate to do this, but I'm going to have to charge you an additional hazard fee."

Corabelle didn't even blink. "Whatever you need."

"By the way," I said, "I didn't see anything on Todd's parents in the information you gave me. Have you talked to them? Do you think they might know something?"

Corabelle shook her head. "No parents. Todd was a ward of the state. He got scholarships for college."

Wow. Aside from the disappearing act, Todd was looking more and more impressive. He'd become a pre-med all on his own. But then again, what did I know? A "ward of the state" could mean anything. I didn't have any parents either.

"Here, in case it helps." I took the photo Corabelle handed me. It was Todd, posing in a body-builder stance under a big tree. Based on the landscape around him, I guessed it had been taken on the same outing as the photo of Corabelle I'd seen in his bedroom. "He didn't want to stand like that," Corabelle told me. "That's why he's making that goofy face. Isn't he cute?"

"Very cute," I agreed. She watched as I scribbled notes. When I looked back up, I noticed her lower lip was cracked from where she'd been biting it. I pulled a tiny container from my pocket. "Do you want some lip balm?"

"No!" Corabelle recoiled as if I'd offered her a dog turd. "Gross!"

"Lip balm is gross?"

"*Sharing* lip balm is gross," she informed me before walking away.

I watched her disappear down the hall. She was willing to make out with almost any healthy male over the age of fifteen, but sharing lip balm was gross? Maybe this was the sort of distinction you formed when you had parents. Like I said, what did I know?

I DIDN'T SEE SKY again until Greek Mythology, which was fine with me. After the previous night's breakdown, I felt way too vulnerable. But I had a plan: our interactions from here on out would only be about Corabelle's case. Nothing about our pasts, nothing about our personal lives. Only the case.

I slid into my seat right as the bell rang, so it was easy to dispense with conversation. When I nodded in Sky's direction, he gave me a brief head jerk: the international sign for "'Sup?"

Fine. Judging from that evidence, he very obviously wanted to avoid me too. Perfect. Just . . . perfect.

Mr. Lowe started off with a homework assignment. He claimed it would be simple. All we had to do was pick a character from Greek mythology who we felt was representative of ourselves, write the name on an index card, and turn it in Wednesday morning. He even gave us the index cards. No biggie . . . except for those of us who happened to be on a (fake) paranormal case and

fake

didn't have time to research a bunch of (fake) mythological people. When the bell rang, I briefly considered texting Norbert to ask him to come up with someone but decided that giving him busywork might be pushing my luck.

So my "To Do" list now included the following: research Greek character, pay electricity bill, find and send Mom's actual birth certificate to my father.

Oh, and locate a missing pre-med student, determine who sent the obituary, and figure out if I actually had a sister.

I only had so many brain cells. Since I needed money, Todd Harmon had to come first.

After class, Sky fell into stride beside me in the hall. "Are you all right? I was worried after last night."

"I'm fine." I stopped and turned to him. "It never happened. Okay?"

"Fine," said Sky. He hitched his backpack up and grasped me by the elbows. Against my better judgment, I allowed him to crowd me into a corner by the wall of lockers. He gazed down at me. For the first time, I noticed that his eyelashes were really long. It pissed me off: both the eyelash length and the fact that I noticed.

"Look," he said. "I get that you're not happy about me barging into your life. Fine. But it's not about me anymore. It's not about what I want."

"Agreed," I said.

For reasons I cannot fathom, my eyes wandered to his mouth.

It was a nice mouth.

"It's about Corabelle," the nice mouth said.

Right. Corabelle.

I pulled away, glaring down a pair of hussies-in-training who were ogling him from behind. Enough.

"Meet me after school at the sundial," I ordered, and left him standing there.

AFTER SUFFERING THROUGH THE rest of the day, I found that my new partner was not alone. Norbert was at the sundial with him. Not just *with* him, but engaged in serious conversation. I marched over to them, hands already on my hips. "What are you guys doing?" I barked.

"Working on the case," Sky said without looking up.

True, I'd already accepted that this would happen, that Sky and Norbert would keep communicating, especially if either felt I was withholding. But accepting it and witnessing it were two different things. "I told you to stay away from my cousin—"

"It's cool," Norbert told me. I opened my mouth to remind him that his definition of "cool" was out of sync with the rest of the world's, but stopped. I had to pick my battles.

"Okay, fill me in," I said with a sigh.

"Fifth period was computer class," Norbert explained before going on a two-minute tangent that involved words like "firewall" and "codes" and "security." The upshot was that Norbert had run Todd's license plate number through the DMV and police department and had discovered something interesting.

"He drives an eight-year-old Honda Accord," Norbert

said. "Teal. He bought it from a used-car lot in Crenshaw last year. Got a fairly good deal on it. High mileage but a low financing fee."

"Is this relevant?" I asked.

"Not at all. I'm just showing off my dope investigative skills."

I stole a peek at Sky. He looked amused.

"But here's the relevant part," Norbert said. "Friday afternoon, the Accord was towed from a no-parking zone downtown."

"Do you have the exact address?" asked Sky.

"No, but I have the location of the tow yard. Clean Lee's off Spring Street."

Sky and I exchanged a glance.

"We'll drop you home first," I told Norbert.

Disappointment crossed his face. He looked at Sky.

"I'll keep her out of trouble," Sky promised. Norbert rolled his eyes, but nodded.

"Stay by your computer in case we need you," I ordered, maybe a little tersely. I couldn't help it. Because mostly I was wondering if he could sense my relief that I wouldn't have an audience—_him_—for the tragicomedy that was my nonrelationship with Sky Ramsey.

IT TOOK SIXTY MINUTES to get downtown, an hour defined by heavy traffic and heavier silence. I couldn't stop thinking about the sister I might have. Part of me wanted to mention the obituary to Sky. I burned to talk about it with someone, but there was no way to bring it up casually. And given Sky's beliefs in the paranormal, I couldn't imagine what sort of crazy response it might trigger. Anyway, it wasn't part of the new plan. The new plan was to talk about the case and only the case.

At long last we rumbled into a bumpy gravel lot.

I pulled out my phone. "Just a sec," I said, tapping a quick message to Norbert:

do me a favor, k? make a list of any former clients who might have been less than satisfied w umbra. thx

It was within the realm of possibility that someone had realized they'd been conned and sent the obituary as retribution. Certainly more possible than anything else that I'd conceived of. I pressed SEND and turned to Sky. "Okay, how do you want to play this?"

"Let's wing it."

Before I could protest, Sky had already leapt from the car and was heading toward Clean Lee's office. Cursing him, I followed at a run.

You wouldn't expect the office of a downtown tow yard to be a glamorous affair, and you would be correct. The room was tiny and filthy and dim. A middle-aged man in a suit as gray as the walls looked up when we entered. "What kind of car?" he demanded.

"Pardon me?" asked Sky.

"What kind of car did you lose?" he said, this time more loudly.

"Actually, we're not here for a car," said Sky.

We're not?

"You're not?" said the man.

Sky stuck out his hand with such confidence that the man shook it automatically. "I'm Sky Ramsey."

"Babe Lee."

"Nice to meet you, Mr. Lee." Sky gestured toward me. "And this is my assistant—"

"Murgatroyd Smith," I said: punishment for calling me his assistant.

Mr. Lee grimaced at me. "Really?"

"Really."

"Your parents are mean," said Mr. Lee.

"Your name is Babe," I retorted.

"My parents are fans of major league baseball," he explained.

Fair enough.

"We're writing an article for the UCLA student newspaper," said Sky.

"So?" said Mr. Lee.

"It's about top local businesses," said Sky. I crossed my arms. I couldn't wait to see how this related back to Todd Harmon's car.

Mr. Lee brightened. "Yeah?"

Sky nodded. "Your company was nominated to be featured. Are you willing to give me a couple quotes, maybe some information about how you got started and why you're so popular?"

Mr. Lee gestured across the dank room to a cluster of dented folding chairs. "Be my guest! I have lots to say about my popularity."

I started toward a chair. Fine. I'd figure out how to work this angle. Maybe open with a question about the most common makes of cars that got towed, then somehow move the conversation toward Hondas . . . But Sky clearly had other plans.

"Murgatroyd, I am conducting the interview," he snapped. He turned to Mr. Lee with an apologetic head-shake. "She's always overstepping her boundaries." Before I could even glare at him, he said, "Just go outside. Get some photos of the exterior. Don't forget shots of the cars." He turned to Mr. Lee. "She can get into the yard, right?"

"Gate's open."

Nicely done. Pretty brilliant, in fact. I had to give Sky that. I threw an appreciative glance at him—he winked in return—and I hurried from the building. It wasn't too hard to find a teal Honda Accord among the dozens of cars packed into the yard. I checked the license plate against the number Norbert had given me. Todd Harmon's car, all right.

Unfortunately, all four doors were locked.

I leaned against the driver's side window and shaded my eyes with my hand to peer inside. There was a backpack on the floor in the back. I was contemplating smashing the window with a rock when I realized there was also some-thing on the front passenger seat. I went around the car to take a look. Lying there were a dozen roses that had—I think—once been red. Now they were brown and brittle, pink tissue paper crumpled around them. A rectangular card lay next to the dead blossoms, blank except for a preprinted message: I LOVE YOU. And underneath that, in small italicized font, the name of the florist: Howard's Flowers.

A quick web search gave me the address.

TEN MINUTES LATER, WE were back in my car and heading toward the Valley. I handed my phone over so Sky could see the photo I'd taken. "Todd bought a bouquet of roses but never gave them to anyone."

"Weird," he mused.

"Roses are expensive," I said. "They're not like chrysanthemums. They're not like Gerber daisies."

"I like Gerber daisies," said Sky.

"Me too," I said. "But they're cheap."

"You're low maintenance. That's nice."

I ignored his comment. "Todd might have bought those roses for Corabelle, but he also could have been planning to give them to some other girl. We know he canceled his date with Corabelle on Wednesday night."

"We know more than that," Sky said. "We know he smelled like hellfire on Thursday morning. We also know that he drove downtown sometime between Thursday night and Friday afternoon."

"And got his car towed," I finished. "We need to figure out where he was heading. Right now, the last time we've been able to definitely place him is at his own apartment on Thursday night. Sometime between when everyone went to bed and when Corabelle woke up on Friday morning, he left and nobody knows where he was going. It could have been anything. A drug score, a booty call—"

"A *succubus* booty call."

I tried very hard not to roll my eyes. I was mostly successful. "Anyway, we need to find out who Todd was going to see downtown."

"It's whoever he met on Wednesday," said Sky.

"You don't know that."

"By all appearances, until he ran into a succubus, he was really into Corabelle."

"People lie," I said.

"Cynic," Sky said, but he laughed, and I couldn't help but laugh too.

"Meeting a succubus on Wednesday is the only reason that makes sense," Sky went on. "Why else would Todd have canceled his date with Corabelle that night? He would have been all hellsick."

"Hellsick," I repeated. "Listen to yourself."

"And tormented," he added, ignoring my comment. "So Todd spent the night like that. Desperate. Suffering. He tried to shake it off and have a normal breakfast with Corabelle. Except he couldn't be normal because he'd already been infected. So he didn't talk to her all day, didn't sleep with her that evening, and then at some point in the night or early morning, he couldn't take it anymore. He left to find the succubus."

I kept my eyes on the road. "You know I think that's ridiculous, right?"

"Think whatever you want, but Todd was going downtown for someone."

"That, at least, I can agree with. He either bought those roses for Corabelle or for a new girl he was seeing."

"Or for a succubus," said Sky.

"Whoever they were for, she never got them."

I didn't need to turn my head to know Sky was nodding. "Because before Todd Harmon could deliver them . . ."

I finished the sentence for him. "He disappeared."

ELEVEN

Howard's Flowers was in Sherman Oaks on Ventura Boulevard between a 99¢ Store and a McDonald's. When Sky and I walked in, Howard was nowhere to be found. Unless, of course, the slim, pig-tailed girl behind the counter was Howard. Which I doubted, since her nametag said she was Susan.

"Can I help you?" she asked us.

"We're looking for information about one of your customers from last week," I said, stepping in front of Sky. Yes, he had done a good job at the tow yard. But this was still *my* case. I was in charge.

"Why?" said Susan.

"We're private investigators," said Sky from behind me.

Susan looked both of us over. "Really?"

"*Junior* private investigators," said Sky.

"The customer's name is Todd Harmon," I told her, trying to sound as old beyond my years as possible.

"He came in on Wednesday," said Sky.

"*Maybe* on Wednesday," I said.

Susan wrinkled her nose like she was thinking really hard. "I was here on Wednesday. I worked almost every day last week because Tori had to take some time off. She caught scabies from her boyfriend."

Apparently Susan had no problem handing out information. But that was fine. It was actually good for our purposes. *My* purposes.

"Sorry about your friend," said Sky.

"Oh, she's not my friend," said Susan. "She's a skanky ho."

For once, it appeared that Sky didn't know how to respond. I jumped in. "Speaking of skanky hos, we think this Todd Harmon guy has one on the side."

"Assface," said Susan.

"He bought a bouquet of roses from your store."

With a shake of her head, Susan dove beneath the counter and came up with a vinyl bag. She unzipped it and rummaged around until she found a wad of credit card receipts held together with a paper clip. She started to flip through them. "Sorry, this is Wednesday's pile, but there's nothing here from Todd Harmon."

"Maybe it wasn't Wednesday," I said.

"Maybe he paid cash," said Sky.

I showed Susan the photo of Todd that Corabelle had given me.

"Does he look familiar?"

"Yep," said Susan. "I remember him."

"You do?" Sky and I said in unison.

Susan went back to the nose-wrinkling thing for a moment before reopening the vinyl bag. She pulled out another wad of flimsy papers. "It wasn't Wednesday," she said.

Of course I couldn't restrain myself from giving Sky a smug look.

"It was Thursday morning. I remember because Wednesday night I had a blind date with this douchey actor guy who was my cousin Monica's friend from grad school," Susan said. "He brought three sheets filled with teeny-tiny photos of himself. Head-shot proofs. Our entire date was spent drinking gasoline prairie fires and looking at those damn pictures of him."

I blinked at her. "And Todd Harmon was—"

"There were so many pictures. So many. I'm telling you, it was the worst blind date in the history of bad blind dates."

"Suck," I said.

"Big suck," Susan agreed. "And to make it worse, I forgot to set my cell phone alarm, so I woke up late, and then didn't know where I was. Did I mention he lived in Manhattan Beach?"

I needed to take control of the conversation, but it was difficult. "You spent the night with him?" I found myself asking.

"I had a _lot_ of gasoline prairie fires. Anyway, I lucked out because Thursday morning traffic wasn't too bad. I got to work only fifteen minutes late, but there were already a couple customers waiting at the door. One of them was Todd Harmon."

"Are you sure?" I asked.

Susan slipped a receipt out of Thursday's bundle and fluttered it at me. "Look."

Sure enough, there was Todd Harmon's autograph,

along with proof that he had paid way too much for a dozen red roses.

I forced myself to smile at Susan. "You have a great memory."

"Actually, I don't. It's just that he was kinda chatty. He told me all about his girlfriend. He was supposed to see her the night before—when I was on my awful blind date—but he had to cancel at the last minute because he had a migraine."

Sky elbowed me. "A migraine?" he asked.

"Yeah. I bet it was more fun than my date. He bought the flowers because he was meeting his girlfriend for breakfast and wanted to apologize for blowing her off. After my crappy-ass night, it was kinda nice to hear a guy talk about how much he likes his girl. I bet *he* never made her sit through a zillion pictures of himself."

"Did he smell funny?" asked Sky.

I shot him a look, but Susan seemed to think that this was a perfectly reasonable question. Maybe lots of funky-smelling people came in there. "I don't think so," she said. "I didn't sniff him, but he *looked* like the kind of guy who would smell good."

I held my phone over the pile of receipts. *Click.*

"Thanks for your time," I told Susan, grabbing Sky's arm and hauling him toward the door.

If he thought we were going to question Susan about the scent of brimstone, he was very wrong. Once outside, I let go of him so I could fire off a quick text update to Norbert before checking my watch. Just enough time to get to the Los Angeles Department of Water and Power service

fake

center to pay my electric bill in cash—if there was zero traffic. Or if I suddenly learned how to fly.

It was shaping up to be another candlelit evening.

When I reached my car, Sky was no longer at my side. He was standing on the sidewalk, looking up and down Ventura Boulevard.

"Hey!" I yelled. "What are you doing?"

He jogged back toward me. "No gas stations nearby," he said.

"I'm not following."

"Todd has to have gone somewhere *after* buying the flowers but *before* he met Corabelle at the restaurant. I was thinking maybe he stopped for gas or something. I wish we'd checked to see how full his tank was at the tow yard."

"And still not following."

Sky sounded overly patient. "He wasn't hellsick here, but he was by the time he met Corabelle for breakfast. He had to run into the succubus somewhere in between Howard's Flowers and the restaurant. I'm trying to figure out where."

I shook my head. "Maybe it's the florist herself. Did that occur to you? That little smack-talking chick back there. Maybe *she's* your succubus."

"Don't be silly." Sky's voice was mild. "She's obviously not a succubus."

The ridiculousness never ended. "And how do you know that?"

"Easy. I didn't want to sleep with her. Not even a little."

My fists sprang to my hips. "That's it?" I squawked. "*That's* your litmus test? If you—you, Sky Ramsey—think a

girl isn't hot enough to screw, she can't be a succubus?" I
was more than offended; I was enraged. But part of it was
anger with myself: I couldn't stop my mind from flashing
back to the moment Sky had called *me* beautiful.

Did that mean he wanted to sleep with me? I had never
done The Deed. I hadn't even gotten close. It wasn't that
I wasn't curious; it was that I'd never been curious enough
to actually let some dumb teenaged boy paw all over me.
And, let's be honest, it wasn't like I had dumb teenaged
boys knocking down my door. Not that any of this mattered. My virginity had zero to do with the case.

"Succubi make men desire them," Sky said in a matter-
of-fact tone. "It's how they operate. Once they kiss you,
you've got the taste for them. It's like a personal signature
from that specific succubus. It's not impossible to break
the addiction, but it's not easy. Todd seems like a nice guy.
If it happened at the gas station, the succubus could have
been at the next pump or something. Todd makes a little
small talk with her, and—bam!—suddenly he's under her
spell. It takes a lot of willpower to look away from the eyes
of a succubus."

"But what about the kiss?" I asked.

Sky shrugged. "All she has to do is lean over and kiss
him. Easy. The question is, *where* did this happen?"

I considered. Yes, Sky was insane for believing that
Todd had been zombified by succubus slobber, but clearly
something weird had occurred, because the guy was MIA.
It couldn't hurt to trace Todd's steps back from his disappearance. I motioned toward my car.

"Get in," I said. "I have an idea."

MOMENTS LATER, WE WERE heading north on Sepulveda. Sky was beside me, one finger skimming over the surface of his phone. Corabelle's voice was in my ear.

"It's just east of the freeway," she said through my headset.

"Who got there first?" I asked her. "You or Todd?"

She gasped. "Do you think he was cursed at the restaurant?"

"That's what we're trying to find out," I said, slipping back into Umbra Investigations mode. It felt weirdly comfortable to lie again. Familiar. Easy. "We're trying to place the time and location of the cursing."

"Todd was first," said Corabelle. "When I got there, he was already sitting in a booth, staring out the window. He didn't stand up when I found him, and he didn't kiss me. He *always* kisses me."

I was silent. Maybe there was someone at the restaurant—a waitress or another customer—whom Todd didn't want seeing him with Corabelle. "Have you ever met any of his ex-girlfriends?"

"No."

"Could there be a girl from his past who wants him back?"

Corabelle huffed loudly in my ear. "*Anyone* from his past would want him back. He's *perfect.*"

Barf.

"Of course. Were you—"

"Hold on," Corabelle interrupted me. "Another call. I have to take this." Then she hung up.

I shot a quick glance at Sky. He was on his phone. "Not yet," he murmured.

Our eyes met. "Hurry," I whispered to him. "We're almost there."

As we crossed over Saticoy, I realized I wasn't only annoyed that he was distracted. I had an unpleasant flickering of jealousy, wondering whom he might be talking to. Sky shook his head at me. "I need something from you," he said into his phone. "Todd's signature."

Conveniently, the light at Stagg turned yellow, so I was able to slam on my brakes. I whirled to face Sky. "Are you freaking kidding me? You called Corabelle while you knew I was talking to her?!"

Sky held a hand in front of my face to shush me while he continued his conversation. "Yes. We're establishing a timeline and need to match it to a receipt from Thursday morning." He paused. "Howard's Flowers." Another pause. "A dozen red roses."

I couldn't hear her response, but I assumed it involved a lot of crying because Sky started saying things like "It's okay" and "I know, I know."

The light turned green. I gunned through it. "I need help navigating if we're going to crack this case!" I said, loudly enough for Corabelle to hear.

Sky made a face at me. "Thanks. I'll be in touch." He hung up. "She has a card that Todd sent her, but it's in her car. She'll text it in a minute."

"And why do you want his signature?" I demanded. "Or a better question: Why didn't you think to tell *me* you wanted it?"

"I want to match it to the one on the receipt for the flowers," Sky explained, slipping back into that overly patient tone. "Maybe we've been going about this in the wrong way. Maybe Todd was already hellsick when he arrived at the florist and Susan missed the smell. After all, she was hungover from a night of gasoline prairie fires and . . . worse." He pointed. "There."

I turned left on Roscoe and pulled into the parking lot of the WaffleVille Diner. Not exactly cheery. There was a faded green awning and an even more faded green roof with peeling paint. It looked as if it was headed for foreclosure.

"Classy place for a date," I said to Sky. "But I still don't understand *why* you want Todd's signature."

"Because," he explained, throwing open the car door, "if Todd was already hellsick at the florist, his signature will be shaky and messy. It's worth comparing to his regular one, right?"

I frowned as we walked toward the diner. Despite the ratty exterior, it emitted the kind of smells that made my mouth water. Someone was baking biscuits. I took back my previous judgment.

"I'm not buying it," I said to Sky. "Todd was coherent enough to tell Susan about Corabelle, and Susan was coherent enough to remember it. He couldn't have been hellsick already." I caught myself. "If such a thing as 'hellsick' even existed, that is."

I heard a buzz, and Sky pulled out his cell phone. "Here it is," he said. "Pull up the other one."

I did, and we held our phones together. The signature

on the receipt I'd photographed was messy, that was for sure. But so was the signature on Sky's phone. They were the same. It just so happened that Todd Harmon had bad handwriting. I was relieved the guy was turning out to have at least one flaw. It would have been tremendously unfair if he was a hot, hard-working pre-med student with beautiful penmanship.

"That's that," I said, and started to pull my phone away.

"Hold on," said Sky. He leaned close over my phone and peered at the photo. His breath was warm on my wrist.

"Hey!"

Sky had abruptly nabbed the phone out of my hand and was staring at the tiny screen. "Holy shit," he whispered. "That's the succubus."

TWELVE

As we sped back down Sepulveda, Sky called Norbert and began rattling off information. "Todd Harmon didn't meet the succubus *after* the florist shop. He met her *at* the florist shop. It's the receipt just to the left of Todd's receipt, on the edge of the picture. It looks like the name is Misty Callahan. Maybe you can blow the image up larger. Find out everything you can: her address, numbers, employment. Call as soon as you have any info."

He hung up and turned to me. "It was there. It happened right there in Howard's Flowers."

"How can you possibly think you know that?" Sky waved my phone at me, and I swatted his hand away. "Driving!"

"Black calla lilies," he said. "She bought black calla lilies."

"What the hell is that supposed to prove?"

Sky made a *pfft* sound. "You don't think succubi like *daisies*, do you? It's classic. In the photo, you can see the receipt of the very next customer after Todd. Misty Callahan buying two dozen black calla lilies!"

I shook my head. "No way. Susan would remember if Todd kissed a succubus—a *girl*—in her store. Especially right after telling her his whole love story about Corabelle."

"Susan could have been in the back room, or maybe she went to the bathroom after ringing up Todd. The succubus—"

"Misty," I said.

"Fine, Misty," he said. "She got her flowers, decided Todd looked scrumptious, and wove her spell. That's why Corabelle thought he smelled burnt at breakfast. He had *just* gotten hellsick. He had *just* been taken over by Misty."

I turned back onto Ventura Boulevard. "And you think that's why he didn't give the flowers to Corabelle?"

"Absolutely," said Sky. "He was jacked up on succubus addiction. Couldn't think straight."

I almost laughed. "That condition seems to be going around."

"You'll see," said Sky, very seriously. "We'll ask Susan about the customer who came in right after Todd. If she's tall and gorgeous, we got our girl."

"We live in Los Angeles," I informed him. "Tall and gorgeous is hardly an anomaly." I flipped on my blinker to turn into the parking lot in front of Howard's Flowers. "Hey, if what you're saying is true about the succubi and how they trap their prey and all that, then what's the defense? How would a guy protect himself? Wear a mask? A mouth guard? Be dorky enough that no self-respecting succubus would ever want to lip-lock with him?"

"Another woman's kiss," said Sky.

I made the turn and pulled into a space before looking at Sky. "Excuse me?"

He grinned. "Succubi hate the flavor of other women on their prey." He winked before glancing toward the building. I watched his grin fade away. "Dammit." Only then did I notice what he had. We were the only car in the parking lot. Howard's Flowers had closed for the night.

AN HOUR LATER, I found myself inching off the traffic-clogged highway exit my cousin had directed us to. "This is pointless," I told Sky.

"No it's not," he retorted. "Norbert found a zip code. Don't you trust your cousin?"

"I completely trust my cousin, but I have no idea why *he* trusts *you*. I think you're a wing nut. And going downtown twice in the same day definitely qualifies as insane."

"Turn here."

Whether he was a wing nut or not, I did as he asked. We drove in silence for a few more minutes. We had already been over and over the *facts*: even though Todd had brought the roses with him, he hadn't given them to Corabelle at breakfast. We'd also been over and over what Sky *suspected*: Todd had been confused and dizzy with succubus addiction, and so the bouquet had lain, forgotten, on his passenger seat while he'd struggled through his meal with Corabelle, his day at work, and an evening at his apartment.

I had to admit: I was having a hard time coming up with a plausible explanation that carried weight in the real world. I ran scenarios through my head: Todd had inexplicably gone on a spontaneous camping trip with a friend who owned equipment. Possible. Todd had fallen suddenly and tragically ill and was on his deathbed somewhere. Improbable, but I made a mental note to have Norbert search local hospital databases, just in case. Or maybe Todd *had* fallen for Misty Callahan, who was only a regular girl in a florist shop, albeit a girl with unusual taste in flowers. But maybe that was it. Maybe it was love at first sight, and Todd didn't know how to tell Corabelle the truth.

"Do you believe in love at first sight?" I blurted out.

"No." Sky's voice was quiet. I assumed he'd repeat the question back to me, but instead there was a long silence. One in which I couldn't bring myself to look at him. One in which all I wanted to do was look at him.

I kept driving.

Sky pointed me to another street and then another. I followed his directions down a sketchy looking block and into a parking structure. I pulled into a space. We hopped out.

"Now what?" I asked. Maybe it was because I had been in charge of everything in my life for so long, or maybe it was because I had an impossible case and an obituary looming over my head—not to mention an unpaid electric bill—but letting someone else make a decision or two was actually a relief.

"Come on," said Sky.

I followed him. We walked out to the street—lightly fragrant with urine, how lovely—and turned onto South Broadway. We passed two Spanish-language churches and

fake

several discount electronics stores. I caught a glimpse of my reflection in one of their windows. Even from the sidewalk, I could see that I was in disarray. My ponytail hung askew. My face was drawn, my eyes ringed with dark circles.

I glanced over at Sky who—of course—looked freshly showered and perfect despite a day of school and investigations. He seemed like the kind of guy who could run a marathon and still smell good afterward. I tore my eyes away from him and stared down at my boots.

A block up, the cement sidewalk gave way to a big, star-patterned mosaic in red and yellow and green. We were crossing it when Sky caught me by the elbow and gave a gentle tug, pulling me toward the adjoining building. We were underneath the awning; my nose told me that we were heading into a restaurant. I stopped moving. "Why are we going in here?"

"Because your stomach growled," said Sky.

Color rose to my cheeks. "No, it didn't."

"Yes it did," said Sky. "In the car."

I managed a smile. Okay, he was right. I'd thought the radio had drowned it out, but apparently Sky had ears like a rabbit.

"I could hear it over your terrible music," he teased.

"My music isn't terrible. It's catchy. That's its genius. But for the record, you are not in charge of feeding me."

"Someone needs to be. Now come on." I let him pull me toward the double glass doors. "Besides," he added, almost too quietly for me to hear, "it's a great restaurant for a first date."

THIRTEEN

It figured Sky would choose this place. It was a smug and subtle jab, at *me*. Right inside the front doors was a forest wonderland. Painted trees and rock formations sprung all the way up to the second floor. A waterfall—with actual water—bubbled down from above. A life-size bear held a plate.

The restaurant was to nature what I was to paranormal detection: totally fake.

Sky guided me into a cafeteria line. The food didn't look fancy, but it smelled fantastic. He knew my taste. We each picked up a dessert (for some reason, they were first), and then I heaped a plate full of sautéed mushrooms and buttered peas and candied yams and added a big yeasty-smelling roll. He got roast beef and mashed potatoes. I reached the cashier before Sky did, but it was too late.

I was fishing through my wallet when I realized he was handing a card over. I turned to scowl at him, but he was already scowling back at me, perfectly mimicking what I'd spent years perfecting.

"See what you look like?" he said.

I laughed. I couldn't help myself.

"You have a nice laugh," he said.

My mouth clapped shut. He should have known by then that I didn't do compliments.

In silence, I followed him up a set of worn stairs to a small balcony with two empty tables. We set our trays down and sat in the vinyl-covered chairs overlooking the main seating area. I took a moment to soak in the kitsch. There were garlands of ivy cascading from fake outcroppings of rock. A giant moose head gazed out from a patch of fake pine trees. Nearby, a tiny open cabin was fronted by a stream lit in brilliant green.

I turned to Sky. "Where did you find this place?"

"Online when I was getting ready to move to Los Angeles. Isn't it cool?"

"I mean, I don't know if 'cool' is exactly the word I'd use . . ."

"But interesting, right?"

I nodded. "Definitely interesting."

Sky started eating. I did the same. I couldn't stop thinking about that word, *date*. Was that what this was? I'd always imagined I would at least shower and change my clothes before a date. Whatever a "date" even was (the mah-jongg-sponsored movie with Michael Wilkins didn't count). I'd spent the entire day with this guy, mostly annoyed at him, but occasionally grateful for his assistance. It was definitely not the normal lead-up to a first date, so how was this supposed to work? What did regular teenagers talk about on dates? *Hey, so I got this obituary that says I'm going to bite it in six months.*

More important, I wasn't convinced that Sky wanted to be on a date with *me*. It was very possible that this was all part of some larger plan I still wasn't seeing: cozying up to the daughter of Dr. Lewis Cade—the daughter he'd black-mailed, no less—for unknown reasons. Maybe he was so persistent because he really did want me to believe in my father's nonsense. Maybe he *was* trying to save me in his own deluded way.

Most important: I'd strayed from the plan.

This dinner had nothing to do with the case.

The silence stretched beyond awkward into excruci-ating as we both finished our dinners.

Finally, as I reached for my strawberry pie, Sky spoke up.

"Now do you want to talk about it?"

I took a bite and made a show of savoring it. "Sure," I said. "It's sweet. And a little tangy."

"Ha-ha," said Sky. "I mean about last night. About your dad, or your mom, or whatever."

My sister.

I fixed my eyes on a cartoonish moon painted on the wall high over the restaurant floor. "Nope."

"Well, too bad," said Sky. "I'm bored of talking about Corabelle's case and thought I'd try regular old chat-ting."

Which, obviously, I suck at. But whatever. I could indulge him with some light conversation, at least for a minute or two.

"Okay, where do you live?" I cringed at my own ques-tion. Would Sky think I was planning to stalk him back, the way he'd stalked me? If that was my best attempt at conversation, I might never have a second date in my whole life. *If* this was even a first one.

"Woodland Hills," he said, pretending not to notice my discomfort.

"Then why don't you go to Taft High School?"

Sky fiddled with his napkin. "I toured it when I moved here and didn't like it."

"Where did you move from?"

"San Francisco."

"Why?"

"Dad got transferred." Sky laid his napkin on his plate. "What do you think Todd was doing downtown?"

Great. My stab at conversation had already failed. So much for regular old chatting. But this was what I wanted anyway, right? This was *good.*

"I don't know," I said, "but do you really, honestly—I mean, *truly*—believe that he fell under the spell of a succubus?"

Sky pushed his plate away and leaned across the table. "Look, Jillian . . . I know you're a skeptic. But don't tell me you've *never* experienced something you can't explain."

I stared back, not sure how to answer. My entire life was an experience I couldn't explain. I had grown up in a house where everything I *thought* I knew turned out to be a lie, a place where the earth shifted under my feet and the rules kept changing. All I knew for certain was that the magic had splintered around me, my mother had gotten lost in the twisted maze of her own mind, and my father had run away on a fruitless quest for something that didn't exist: answers.

Or maybe that's just what you tell your kid when you abandon her.

Sky didn't push me. He waited for me to answer, to form my thoughts. Where to start? There was so *much* that didn't make sense. Memories swam up from my childhood: murky, impossibly tall shapes looming over my bed at night. *My parents checking on me.* Whispers in a language I didn't know. *A babysitter from another country.* Shadows that could only be glimpsed in passing. *Figments of my overactive imagination.*

The way Mom used to twitch her fingers and make the laundry dance on the clothesline.

"It was the wind." I didn't realize I'd said it out loud until Sky responded.

"What?"

I swallowed, hard. "Nothing."

Sky leaned even closer. "Jillian, you're different. Special. You've always known it." Once again, he sounded as if he were pleading with me. Only this time, I knew that he was right. I didn't know how he knew it, but Sky Ramsey was right. There *was* something different about me.

Something broken.

"No!" The word popped from my mouth like a firecracker. I shoved my chair back from the table. "I'm done."

I stalked out of the balcony, down the stairs, and across the restaurant to the door without looking back. Not that I had to. Sky was right behind me. He followed me all the way to my car.

FOURTEEN

We were back on the case. Just like I wanted. Sky poked at his phone, occasionally giving me directions, and I drove. Other than that, neither of us said a word, which was fine with me. As the sun set and the city streetlights glowed to life, Sky and I were back to our normal, totally abnormal, routine.

We ended up in Little Tokyo. I had never been there before, so I wasn't prepared for the cool and funky factor. Lots of neon and signs written in what I assumed was Japanese. A woman in a red kimono walking a tiny dog, also in a red kimono. Bars and tattoo parlors and more skinny jeans than I'd ever seen in one place. What I did *not* see was either Todd Harmon or a succubus.

"I assume you're logging on to your account at wild-goosechase.com," I said to Sky, finally shattering the silence. Sometimes I amuse myself with my own wit. Sometimes I have to in order to survive.

Sky shook his head. "Nope, just trying to find places that might be fronts for a succubus hangout. Do you want me to delete your spam?"

I craned my neck to see what he was looking at. "Wait, is that *my* phone? Why are you on my phone? Get out of my email!"

"Relax. I was checking to see if Norbert sent anything else." He made a mock *tsk-tsk* sound. "Although someone is really concerned that you're not satisfying your partner—"

"Stop it." I reached over and snatched my phone out of his hands, nearly causing us to swerve onto the sidewalk. I straightened out the car. "We're done. This isn't getting us anywhere."

"Sure it is," he countered. "We're narrowing down our options."

"By cruising around Little Tokyo and looking for places where female demons hang out?"

Sky nodded. "Look for bars with 'fire' in the name. Or 'moon.' Or 'smoke.'"

"Or 'delusional'?"

Suddenly Sky grabbed my arm. "Pull over!"

I skidded to the curb in front of a club with a blazing sign out front: FULL MOON. Silhouettes of overly busty women were painted on the windows.

"Sorry, never mind," said Sky. "Girly bar."

"Can we be done now?" I asked. But even as I said it, I knew I didn't completely want the night with Sky to be over. His questioning, his intensity, his insistence that I was different—it might all have been part of an act, but it wasn't enough to scare me away. After all, I was accustomed to acts. I had grown up in a sideshow world, and most of the time, I was still living there. The way Sky danced on the edge of truth—it felt familiar. Comfortable.

Normal.

And—let's be honest—there was something about the way his messy blond hair fell over his forehead.

Sky snapped his fingers. "Hold on." He picked up his own phone and started stabbing at the screen.

"What are you looking for?"

"Vampire clubs. I know, I know, it's not succubi, but websites—crowd-sourced reviews or something—they might not know the difference." He ran his finger down the list he'd pulled up. "The Iron Bar . . . Toothy Dance Den . . . Blood Lust . . ."

"Fang You Very Much."

Sky frowned, scanning the screen. "Where do you see that?"

"It was a joke." I exaggerated his frown back at him.

He broke into a smile. "Good one." He held my gaze a second too long before turning back to his phone. "Here!" he said, tapping the screen. "If that's not a succubus bar, I don't know what is."

I nodded. "Let's go."

I SHOULD HAVE CALLED it a night, but I didn't. Maybe I wanted answers about Todd Harmon for Corabelle's sake. Maybe I was happy to be distracted from thoughts of the obituary, from the sister I might have. Maybe I couldn't help myself because I was already falling for this mysterious, green-eyed boy who believed in all the nonsense my father had built a career on.

Or maybe I just didn't want to go back home to an empty, dark apartment.

At the very least, I thought following Sky Ramsey couldn't hurt.

But as I found out later, everything to do with Sky Ramsey could hurt.

It could hurt a lot.

FIFTEEN

The club at the far end of the alley was marked only by a hand-painted sign over a door: LILITH'S BED. There was a moon over the lettering. Sky nudged me. "Lilith is supposed to be one of the originals," he said. "It's a succubus bar, all right."

The nearby streetlights were out. Honestly, it was a little eerie. I turned to Sky. "I don't suppose you happen to have a fake ID on you."

"Nope. But I can't imagine this is a place that strictly follows the rules." His eyes traveled down my body and back up again. By the time they had reached the level of my own gaze, heat was rising in my cheeks. I covered the only way I knew how.

"Seen enough?" I snapped.

"Just trying to figure out if they'll let you in." He nodded toward my car. "What do you have in the way of costumes?"

I opened the back door and made a sweeping gesture toward my stockpile of thrift store items. "Knock yourself out."

A few moments later, Sky emerged. He'd spread some clothes out on the seat, but it was too dark to identify any item in particular. "Don't take this the wrong way," he said, "but you actually already kinda look like you belong in a succubus bar."

That brought me up short. Did he mean that I looked like a succubus, and if so, was it a compliment? And did it mean he wanted to sleep with me? I was positive that in all the history of uncertain teenage relationships, there had never been one so fraught with questions as this *thing* between Sky and me.

Sky cocked his head to the side, looking over my ripped jeans and black boots. "Your shirt could be sexier. You know, so you look like you dressed up to go to a club." I squinted down at my black T-shirt. It was formfitting and emblazoned with one word written in yellow block letters: HATER.

"Do you have a suggestion?" I asked.

"How about scissors?"

"I have a pocket knife."

Five awkward minutes later, the size of my shirt's neck hole had been greatly increased, and the sleeves were nonexistent. The shirt now fell off one shoulder. I had a moment of gratitude when I realized I'd worn my pretty red bra and not one of the ratty old tan ones. Sky helped me yank the shirt material to the side so we could knot it against my torso. His knuckles grazed my skin, and I hoped he wouldn't register the goose bumps rising to the surface.

When a good-sized slice of my midriff was visible, Sky reached toward my head. I pulled away.

"Come on," he said. "Just a little adjustment."

Fine.

I held still as he gently tugged the rubber band from around my ponytail. My hair tumbled down like a messy waterfall. Before I could reach up to compose it, he had already slid both hands past my cheekbones and into the tangled strands. I froze, staring up at him. I think he was supposed to be doing whatever one does to hair—fluffing it or something—but instead his hands curved around to cradle my head, his fingers moving in gentle circles against my scalp. It was dark, but not so dark that I couldn't tell when his eyes drifted down to meet my own. He swallowed and pulled away.

Something clenched inside me. Something I didn't understand. Sky was charming but arrogant. Helpful but misguided. Smart but naïve. He was maddening. Yes, I was attracted to him, but I couldn't trust him. He'd black-mailed his way into my life, and I still didn't understand his end game. Which somehow *fed* the attraction . . .

Maybe I was mad at *myself.*

Suddenly I realized Sky was unbuttoning his own shirt. All the way. "What are you doing?" My question came out more harshly than I'd intended.

"We're about to walk into a succubus bar," he answered, yanking one arm and then the other out of his sleeves. Resolutely, I kept my eyes on his face and not anywhere near his now-naked torso. "We need to make everyone believe that I'm a present."

My eyes narrowed. "A present?"

"A gift. From you to the succubus. You're going to tell

her that you want to be her disciple, that you're hoping to learn at her lair."

I wasn't sure how I was supposed to respond. "This is helping us find Todd how?"

"Because he's probably already there. In her lair." Sky once again spoke as if he were addressing a bright and well-meaning toddler, the tone he always seemed to adopt when frustrated with my lack of Dr. Lewis Cade pseudoknowledge. "We know she likes young guys. You offer me to her, and she'll tell us the location."

"Are succubi stupid?" I asked.

"Quite the opposite."

"Then why would she tell us where her lair is?"

Sky sighed. "Because we're going to slip her some truth serum." He tossed his shirt into my car. "Do you have a belt in there?"

My grasp on the situation was growing tenuous. I felt as if I were missing chunks of the conversation, that I'd tuned in to some bizarre reality TV show halfway through the episode. "No . . . I mean, only this." I hunted around until I found a length of steel chain links I'd picked up at a swap meet. Occasionally I would wear it around my waist and clasp it with a pin made from bent nails. It pretty much screamed badass.

"That is badass," said Sky.

And there it was.

He looped the chain around his own neck and secured it with the rubber band he'd taken out of my hair. He handed the free end to me. Any passerby would think I was walking him like a dog on a leash. I cracked a smile.

"Nice," I said.

"Don't get used to it."

I couldn't help it. I laughed out loud. This whole thing was insane, but hey, if I got to trot into an adult nightclub with Sky Ramsey on a leash . . . I was damn well going to enjoy it. At the very least, it took my mind off other concerns—namely, a sister I didn't know and a death threat in the form of an obituary, both of which may or may not have been real.

We headed down the alley, skirting piles of broken glass and edging between overflowing trash bins and hulking dumpsters that smelled like someone had died inside. Judging from the part of town we were in, maybe someone had. Maybe more than one.

I squinted toward a person outside the club at the end of the alley—a *shape*, really, hidden beneath a hooded cloak, crouched on a stool that looked too small to support its weight. I could hear thudding music beyond the wooden door. As we approached, the shape lifted what I presume was its head. I couldn't see its face, but the voice under the hood was not at all what I expected: silky and high-pitched, with a faint accent I couldn't identify. I couldn't even tell if it was male or female.

"Are you members?" the voice asked.

I glanced at Sky, who was staring straight ahead. He gave an almost imperceptible shake of his head.

"No," I said. "Not members."

The shape held out a hand. It was slender and the skin was a dark, dark brown. The fingernails were cut short and stained black. "Two hundred dollars."

I opened my mouth, but before I could formulate a protest, Sky's arm was already extended. The shape took the wad of bills from his palm and then gestured toward the door. "Enjoy."

I didn't know why Sky had that sort of cash on him, but I decided not to think too hard about it. I decided not to think too hard about anything. If nothing else, this night could go down in history as the world's most expensive and weirdest teenage date (if it was a date?) in history.

I pulled open the door and paused to look at Sky. We didn't say anything. No words were needed.

SIXTEEN

The music—*Goth rock? Black metal? Psycho-industrial?*—was deafening. Beyond deafening. The bass throbbed into my heels. It pounded up my thighs, ricocheted through my torso, and clogged my ears, disrupting my brain, making it impossible to think straight. Now and then, a deep voice moaned lyrics I couldn't understand. It sounded like the kind of music I might tell people I liked while secretly listening to the cheesy pop I really *did* like.

Far above us, a midnight ceiling was pricked with lights. Torches burned on the walls (clearly fire codes were not a concern here). Sweaty, swaying female bodies were everywhere: dancing and smoking and drinking and groping. One woman dressed in what looked like black plastic wrap undulated against a pole. Another, her hands cuffed together, twirled on a trapeze. Everywhere I turned, there were whips and fangs and tattoos and piercings—and cigarettes.

That clinched it: this club was not on any official grid. The cops would have shut it down in a second.

Also: It was hard to feel like a badass here.

I steeled myself, forcing my way deeper into the crowd and tugging Sky along behind me.

There were some men, but not many. They seemed to be mostly clustered around the edges, watching. I peered at the one closest to us. He was slumped to one side, staring out at the dance floor. His fingers twitched at his sides; his eyes were glazed. Drool glimmered at one corner of his mouth.

Hawt.

I had to give Sky this: if there *were* such things as succubi, this totally looked like the kind of horrible nightclub where they'd hang out. I motioned for him to lean over so I could yell into his ear. "So you want me to believe all these girls are succubi?"

He shook his head. "No, most are posers," he yelled back. "It's like the age-old adage: Just because the girl's in black glitter doesn't mean she's a banshee." Several other age-old adages leapt to mind—most of them having to do with being an idiot—but I kept my mouth shut. No use developing laryngitis just so I could insult Sky. He began pointing around, labeling people for me. "Poser, poser, wannabe, supplicant—"

"Whoa." I stopped him. "Supplicant?"

"Like a slave," he explained. "Or a pet. They're girls who worship the succubi. They bring them men, like you're going to do tonight."

I nodded, feigning seriousness. "Where do you throw the twenty-sided dice to find out how many charisma points your orc gets?"

"There's no such thing as an orc," Sky said mildly.

Sky: one. Sarcasm: zero.

"Okay, here's the plan." He leaned in so I could hear him better. "We'll disguise the truth serum in a drink."

Maybe he hadn't ignored the sarcasm. Maybe he was finally joking around himself. "Ah yes, the truth serum," I repeated. "You mentioned it."

"Succubi are notorious liars," Sky explained.

I searched his eyes. Not good. He wasn't joking at all. "I'm guessing you brought the six-pack of truth serum?" I shouted over the music. "I'm fresh out."

"No you're not," said Sky without missing a beat. "Human blood. A tiny bit makes them so drunk they can't help but tell the truth."

"Nice. Well, you're on your own with that one." I curled the end of the belt around my hand and headed toward the bar, yanking him along. I figured it wouldn't be long before we were noticed by regulars, at which point we'd get either threatened or kicked out. But I'd deal with that when it came. I was already here, and frankly, it wasn't so terrible having Sky Ramsey on a leash. Besides, it wasn't like I was worried about getting in trouble with my parents. Freedom from consequences: the only bonus to my family situation.

A chick wearing a glittery green leotard stood behind the counter. She didn't look much older than me. Again I marveled at how so much of Los Angeles didn't seem to care about the law. I waited to see how she'd react to our leash scenario. Her gaze traveled up and down Sky's bare chest, much the way his gaze had traveled up and down my body.

"Tender," she said.

"Thanks," I told her. She looked at me, and I looked at her, and we stood there looking at each other for way too long before I realized she was waiting for me to order.

I wasn't sure what to say. I was in high school, for crap's sake.

Luckily for me, Sky pressed closer from behind. I heard his voice in my ear. "Three drinks," he said. "Something red."

"Three cranberry juices," I said.

The girl looked surprised.

"With vodka," I added hastily.

"Three vodka cranberries. Gimme a sec." She started throwing glasses around and pouring things into other things. Being underage was definitely *not* a problem here. Not that I was surprised. She glanced up at Sky again. "Is he yours?"

"No," I said. "Definitely not." Even as I said it, part of me wondered how it would feel to respond differently, how it would feel if Sky could somehow be defined as *mine*.

I wrestled that part of me into submission and shoved it away.

"Tell her I'm a present for Misty," Sky hissed. "Ask where she is."

Okay then. It was official: I was in Crazy Town. I just had to make myself at home. I leaned further over the bar and jerked a thumb back at Sky. "Actually, he's for Misty," I said. "Know where she is?"

"She doesn't take gifts *here*." The bartender sneered, plopping three glasses of red liquid in front of me.

Huh.

I pulled out some bills and flung them onto the counter. It was the least I could do after Sky dropped two hundred on admission. Then I jerked on the belt so Sky had to step forward. If the bartender thought he was a hottie, maybe showing him off a little would help. I held up my hand and pulled, forcing Sky to pivot. Then, hating it and yet kind of not hating it, I ran my hand down the smooth muscles of his torso.

Dear God.

I managed a tight grin for the bartender. "Misty will want *this*, don't you think?"

Admiration shone from her eyes. "I would." She jerked her chin toward the other side of the cavernous room. "Red throne in the back."

A throne? Seriously?

"Thanks." I passed a cranberry vodka to Sky, took the other two, and struck out onto the dance floor. It was hot. Humid. The music grew louder; it was all-consuming. Around us, bodies were grinding against each other. Lost in the beat, lost in each other.

Sky brought his mouth to my ear. "Good job back there!" he yelled.

"What about the truth serum?" I shouted.

We stumbled into a clear pocket on the dance floor where we were momentarily not in danger of getting hip checked by leather-bound women. Probably good Norbert wasn't around to witness this. He'd have had a heart attack.

"Allow me," Sky shouted back.

I turned to face him. I was holding a drink in each hand,

so I had no way to fend him off when he danced (I use that word loosely) toward me. He set his one free hand on my bare wrist and slid it up my arm to my shoulder. I intended to wriggle away, but somehow I didn't. I stood very still, holding those two drinks, letting Sky trail his fingers up my neck. His index finger traced the outer shell of my ear. I hoped he couldn't feel the involuntary shiver that ran down my spine. He circled my ear lobe. I fought the urge to close my eyes.

He flinched.

I blinked.

When he pulled his hand away, he held it over his drink, squeezing his thumb. A drop of blood fell into the vodka cranberry. I must have pulled The Ultimate Grimace of Ultimate Disgust, because Sky looked amused. "Your earring," he explained at a bellow.

Now it made sense. Really gross sense.

Sky had impaled his thumb on my earring post.

"Yuck," I said. He cupped a hand over his ear and leaned closer. "Yuck!" I yelled louder.

Before I could stop him, he dripped blood into the two glasses I held.

Well, that's one way to prevent underage drinking.

I turned and continued threading my way through the dancers, leading Sky by the neck belt tucked under my arm. Toward the rear of the club, the crowd began to thin out. It was even darker back there—if that was possible—and the torches lining the wall seemed even further away. *Too* far away. The temperature dropped, and everything became a murky shadow.

fake

"Does anything look like a red throne?" I shouted at Sky.

He shook his head. I was about to give up when I felt the belt tug in my hand, making one of the drinks slosh. I turned. Sky was squinting into the distance. I followed his gaze.

There, several tables over and beyond a dark column, was a raised platform. It was outlined by a string of dim lights. A heavy, carved wooden object loomed atop it. The object was definitely chair-like in shape. From where we stood, it was difficult to make out almost any other details, but one thing was certain: it was blood-red.

SEVENTEEN

Her skin wasn't pale in the way people usually say someone's skin is pale. Not like a Caucasian baby's or a redhead's. It wasn't even pale the way milk is pale. It was luminescent, a *glowing* white, like the moon on a clear night, when it is full and low and seems too close to be real. Unreal and otherworldly. And way, way too close.

Sky and I stood at the foot of the platform, staring up at her. She was seated on the wooden throne—the bartender hadn't lied; it was definitely a freaking *throne*—staring down at us. I couldn't get a read on her expression. Maybe I didn't want to. My eyes roved over her outfit: very black and very shiny and very tight, especially her shirt. She looked like her naked body had been painted with ink. Her hands were splayed on the armrests, and her finger-nails were long and red. Carvings of wings rose up by the sides of her head. Beside her, on a high side table, was a vase of flowers.

Black calla lilies.

I took a step closer, Sky lagging behind me on his neck

belt. Misty, the fake succubus, whoever or whatever she was, leaned forward. Her eyes were very dark. I couldn't discern the pupils. I felt as if I were looking into wells with no bottom. Her lips were as red as her fingernails. When she spoke, her voice was the purr of a giant panther. "This is new," she said.

Poser or not, I had to hand it to her: she had the succubus act down.

Sky nudged me from behind. I held one of the glasses up toward Misty. As she accepted it, I caught a glint of a thick gold ring she wore on her left hand. "Am I to consider this an application?" she asked in that throaty animal voice.

Was there a correct answer?

"It's more like a conversation," I finally managed.

I felt those dark eyes scan me. "You're not as deferential as most," Misty said. She held her glass in my direction. "Trade with me."

She wasn't stupid either. She knew we could have put something in her drink. But Sky was sharp too and had foreseen this: the same thing was in *all* the drinks. He poked me in the back, and I raised my glass. A smile flashed over Misty's face, and instead of taking the drink, she clinked her own against it. "To conversation," she said, raising her vodka-cranberry-blood cocktail to her lips.

A test then.

I paused with my glass held out before me. If I actually drank this, it would be the single most disgusting thing I had ever done . . .

In that moment of indecision, Misty's face changed.

Her eyes narrowed to slits and became even darker than before. Her spine straightened. She seemed to grow larger on her throne.

For the first time, a coil of true fear tightened around my abdomen. It occurred to me that it actually didn't matter what *I* believed; Misty herself may have very well believed that she was a real, live succubus. And that made her dangerous. Sky jammed his finger into my back again. I managed a sickly smile. "Cheers," I said, and drained my glass.

Misty did the same.

My drink definitely tasted a lot more like vodka than cranberry. Luckily I couldn't taste any hint of Sky's blood. I didn't know what to do with the now-empty glass. I just held on to it, but Misty flicked hers out in front of the throne. I jumped when it shattered. Behind me, Sky set a calming hand on my lower back.

Misty snapped her fingers toward Sky's drink, then pointed at me. "Indulge," she said. I took the glass from Sky and obeyed in three fast gulps. She leaned toward me. "You would become my disciple?"

I had no idea what she was talking about. It was also suddenly hard to hear her. I searched my muddled brain for an answer. "Your lair," I finally said.

Damn you, vodka!

"You would learn at my lair?" she asked.

I nodded, satisfied I had gotten the right answer.

Misty cocked her head again. Actually, it was more like she *flopped* her head to one side. It seemed like there was something sloppy about it, especially because all her other movements had been so controlled, so precise. Was Sky right? Was that tiny drop of blood taking effect? Or was it the vodka? It was a little difficult to tell when I was so woozy myself.

"Presumptuous," she said, but she slurred a tiny bit. Her eyes traveled past me to fix on Sky. "However, this one is tempting." Her voice now sounded less like a purr and more like oil being poured. Liquid. Thick. I turned to Sky—desperate for any hint about what to say next—but his gaze was locked on Misty. His green eyes were focused and clear, but his lips were slightly parted. I saw him swallow.

Something was wrong.

I edged in front of him, hoping to break his line of sight, but he was much taller than me. His eyes stayed fixed over my head.

"Stop looking at her," I whispered.

"I'm not," he said in a voice that had become flat and dull like a robot's.

And yet he *was*.

I spun back to Misty. She oozed forward in her seat and slowly dripped from the throne. Her eyes slid over to meet mine. I clung to the sobriety I had left, which was enough for me to realize that she looked as wobbly as I felt. "Normally I only accept at my lair in Leimert Park," Misty told me. "But this one appears to be an excellent gift."

Except she said "thish" instead of "this."

"Just the right size." I meant it in a joking way, but my comment made Misty's dark eyebrows knot.

"What do you mean?" she demanded. "Have you befouled this gift?"

"No!" I thought I knew what she meant, but now I was legitimately scared, so I babbled the first thing that came into my head. "Of course not! I wouldn't dream of it. I meant that he seems like someone you would be into. All tall and young like . . ." I paused, not sure if pushing further—while drunk, no less (and why the hell *did* people get drunk, anyway?)—would help or hurt our cause.

Misty drew herself up to her full height and glowered down at me. "Like who?"

Here goes nothing.

"Like Todd Harmon," I whispered.

In a pounce, Misty was off the platform. "Todd Harmon is *mine* now." She trained her eyes on Sky, fusing her gaze to his. The spark in Sky's eyes winked out and was replaced by something I couldn't identify. Maybe because the spark hadn't been replaced. There was . . . nothing. Emptiness.

My fear rose, making my skin tingle. Becoming panic. If Misty really did believe she was a succubus, maybe she knew all sorts of tricks to convince everyone else she was too. Hypnosis. Brainwashing. Mind games too twisted to imagine. Why had I even *come* here? It was the kind of bad choice made by a seventeen-year-old who lived alone. But what was Sky's excuse? He had parents, didn't he? Maybe I *should* have moved in with Norbert and Aunt Aggie and Uncle Edmund. Maybe I was in over my head . . .

Misty took a step toward us, her eyes never leaving Sky's. "There is an energy I am sensing here." She moved closer to him. "Something different."

I should have bolted at that moment. I should have dragged Sky right out of there on his leash. We'd found what we'd come for: this freakish woman had admitted to knowing something about Todd Harmon. We could tell Corabelle we'd made progress. But I couldn't seem to will my body to move. Misty's nearness was terrifying in a way that made no sense. I felt ice in my temples. Electricity crackled down my back. More frightening, Sky seemed to have lost the ability to speak.

I tugged on the neck belt, but he didn't react. Not even a little.

Shit.

Misty was now standing right beside me, staring down at Sky. Yes, down. The chick was *that* tall. I heard a sound like bees buzzing, thousands of them. Panic turned to terror.

She raised her hands to her head and pulled them slowly through the inky strands of her hair. Sky's eyelids were at half-mast, his mouth slack. I could hear his breath. It was coming out hard. Fast. I edged closer to him, and my drunken brain tried to think of a way to distract Misty, to draw her attention back to *me* and away from *him*.

"I don't think you should take . . . uh . . . the gift now," I said. That was my line. I clung to it, hoping against hope that we *were* all just actors in a really screwed-up fantasy, playing parts that should not have been conceived. "A last-minute change of operating procedure is never a good idea." I tripped over the last words.

Misty didn't seem to notice, or even hear me. Her hand shot out with inhuman speed. She caught Sky by the neck belt and jerked him closer. Her mouth twisted into a grinning snarl. There was a flash of gleaming, bone-white teeth. They were model perfect but too *big* somehow. I

fake
∧

grabbed Sky's hand and tugged it, but it was like pulling on a boulder. He didn't budge.

Misty slowly parted those awful white teeth, and I dug my fingernails into Sky's palm. At that moment, I wouldn't have been surprised if smoke had billowed from her mouth.

It wasn't smoke. It was her tongue.

Her long, black, forked tongue.

Time screeched to a standstill. Sky didn't move. He was paralyzed. Frozen. Lost in her spell. Maybe there wasn't a difference.

Something invaded my nose. An unnatural, inhuman stench. The breath of a Jurassic dung beetle. A bomb exploding in an outhouse. A million rotten eggs burning in a dirty oven. And no, it was nothing I had ever smelled before, but I still knew exactly what it had to be. Only one word did it justice. Sky had used it himself.

Hellfire.

Misty leaned down, that horrifying tongue reaching out for Sky, and everything that he had said flashed through my mind—all the crazy things about succubi and addiction and danger. There was only one thing to do, and so I did it. I launched myself between them. I grabbed Sky by the hips and yanked his body into mine, tilting my face upward and sliding one hand up the back of his neck. I pulled his head down and pressed my mouth against his.

Without allowing myself to think, I kissed him. Hard.

And it worked. I felt him respond. I felt his lips open against mine, his hands traveling up my back, folding me into the embrace, entangling me with him . . .

From behind me, I heard a hiss. A loud hiss, loud enough to be heard over the thumping music. I jerked away from Sky. He blinked, as if waking up, and his eyes found mine. They cleared. His mouth formed a word, but I couldn't hear it. I choked for air, trying to steady myself. He said it again. This time, I heard it. This time, it made sense.

The word was *"run."*

EIGHTEEN

The dance floor was even more mobbed than before. Trying to escape was like hacking through a living jungle, a dense tangle of sweaty, writhing vines. Every time I tried to speed up, I found myself caught against another naked torso or glistening bicep or thrusting hip. I kept my legs moving and my eyes on the door.

Sky darted forward and kept a tight hold of my hand as he twisted through the crowd, pulling me with him. We were almost to the edge of the dance floor when he glanced back. I started to turn my head, but he pulled me along. "Come on!" he screamed over the music. We broke free of the crowd, blasted through the tiny antechamber, and shoved open the heavy wooden door to the alley.

It was dark, all shadows. My senses took a moment to readjust. From outside, the music was thankfully muffled, back to a low thud, though that might have been because my ears felt like they were stuffed with cotton.

The security/bouncer/dark-shape person was gone, the stool abandoned. Before I knew what was happening,

Sky grabbed it, flipped it over, and smashed it against the ground. The seat broke off and rolled away.

"What are you doing?" I whispered.

Sky stomped against the stool legs, breaking them apart. He slid two of them between the handles of the door and grabbed my hand again. "Buying us some time."

We started up the darkened alley at a run and were halfway to the street when we heard a giant crashing sound. I whirled to see the club's wooden door fly apart in a hail of splinters. Two impossibly huge men lumbered out through the wreckage and cast their heads about, as if smelling the air.

We slid to a halt. A semitruck had backed into the narrow alley, blocking our exit. My heart jackhammered in my chest. The trailer door was open, the inside compartment filled with boxy silhouettes, but there were no people to be seen.

We were trapped.

"Get behind me," breathed Sky.

The two giant figures swung in our direction. Their heads were large, almost too large for their bodies.

"Descendants of Asterion," Sky said, as if answering my unspoken question. "I'd put money on it."

I glanced at him, suddenly wishing I'd paid more attention to Dad's work, that I'd interrogated Sky more thoroughly about his beliefs—that I'd done a lot of things differently up until this moment. "What does that mean?" I whispered.

"Wait until they charge." He edged backward toward the truck, pushing me behind him as he went. "If we

split up before they hit us, they might not know which
way to go."

"What do you mean 'charge'?" I whispered.

Sky didn't have to answer. The two huge figures lowered their oversize heads and began thundering up the
alley. Actually *thundering*. The ground shook. When one
of them tilted its head back, the roar that came out of its
mouth was a volcano erupting.

We were too far from the semi to try to get inside and
shut the door. There were no convenient fire escapes in the
alley. Even the dumpsters' lids were closed. There was no
way out. There was only me, Sky, and two giants crashing
toward us. When Sky shouted, his voice was far away. I
vaguely registered that he was telling me that I should run
to the left and he'd go right, but I was panicked and horrified and two vodka-cranberry-and-bloods deep.

Instead, I broke free and ran in the craziest direction of
all: straight toward the giants.

In retrospect, I think my feverish plan was to surprise them. Maybe they'd be so shocked that they'd be
stumped. Or if that didn't work, maybe once they saw me
close up, they'd realize I was just a scared teenaged girl.
And I'd see that they were just two ordinary guys with
exceptionally large heads and bodies. They'd take pity
on me. On us. Maybe even escort us back to my car and
check our GPS to be sure we knew how to get back to the
Valley.

Or maybe I was hoping that by running toward them,
I'd wake up from a nightmare and find myself back in my
apartment, gasping for air in bed.

Instead, my foot hit a patch of gravel. I skidded and went down hard on one knee, feeling a sharp twist in my ankle. Behind me, Sky screamed something unintelligible. There was no time to answer. I was about to be trampled. The two terrible shapes blasted straight toward me, on course to shred my body beneath their pounding feet. I tucked my knees into my chest and braced myself against the asphalt. I threw up my hands—as if they could offer any protection—and I . . . *pushed.*

It was instinct. The last desperate move of the condemned. I didn't even know *what* I was pushing. Air. Energy. My impending death.

Of course, neither giant slowed down at all. The one in front whipped right past me, but I was directly in the path of the other. Its feet hit me—at least, they must have hit me, though I didn't feel anything—and it lost its balance, flying over and beyond me, slamming into a concrete wall in a bone-breaking thud.

Then it was still.

I started to scramble up, but everything had turned to jelly: my joints, my muscles, my brain. I was too weak to move. I could only watch as the other giant skidded to a stop at the semitruck's entrance. When he turned around, I finally saw the contours of his face. He had wide, flaring nostrils and eyes that were tiny and focused . . . and furious. As I stared at him, his huge head lowered. One of his immense boots lifted and then dropped, slamming into the ground and scraping across it.

He was preparing to charge. Directly at me.

A gasp formed in my throat. My hands flew to my hips,

feeling for anything in my pockets that could help: a key, a lighter, lip balm, anything at all—

And then the beast disappeared in a deafening crash of jangly chords.

I blinked. My brain scrambled to process the miracle that had just occurred: a massive shape had fallen onto the beast from the semitruck, crushing him into the pavement. A shape that was . . . musical.

Sky jumped out from the truck in the wake of whatever had tumbled out of it. He ran to me. "Come on," he panted with a glance back down the alley. "We don't know who else they'll send after us."

My brain fought to push words out through my mouth. "How?" I managed to say. "What did you do?"

He almost smiled. Then he shook his head. "That's a piano truck. I dropped a piano on him. I didn't think that could happen in real life."

As opposed to all the other "real life" things we've experienced tonight, I thought.

SKY AND I FLED by crawling underneath the truck between its wheels. It was all a bit of a blur until we were on the 101 and heading west. For some reason, with me sitting in the passenger seat.

"Hey!" I squawked, once I got my bearings. "I'm the only one who drives my car!"

"Not when you've been drinking," said Sky.

Fair point. "Well, what about you? Driving after zombification by succubus doesn't seem so wise either."

Sky smiled. I wasn't expecting a smile.

"What?" I said, careful to enunciate the word.

"Oh, nothing," he said. He kept his eyes on the road. "I'm just noting your usage of the word 'succubus.'"

"What about it?"

"You believe me now. You know I've been right all along."

"What I know is . . ." My voice petered out. "What I know is not a whole lot, other than you're a crazy person." I paused, stewing in my passenger seat, thinking back over everything we'd been through in the past few hours. "You don't think they're dead, do you?"

"Who?" asked Sky.

"Those big . . ." I faltered, not sure of the right word to use. "Men."

"No, they're not dead."

"How do you know?"

"It would take more than a piano. Descendants of Asterion are notoriously difficult to kill. Their skulls are pretty much unbreakable. Your dad calls them 'modern day minotaurs.'" Sky shook his head. "Honestly, you don't pay any attention at all to your father's lectures, do you?"

Oh, please.

However, I was glad he'd brought up my father. Because it reminded me that people believed what they wanted to believe. Not just suckers, but people like Misty, people who were very dangerous. There *could* be a rational explanation for everything. For every last part of it.

"FYI, there's such a thing as makeup," I said after a moment.

"Makeup."

"Yeah, makeup. And costumes. And stunt equipment."

Sky flicked the turn signal to head off the highway. "We were both standing right there when Misty got all up in my face. How do you explain her if she's not a succubus?"

"A tongue extender." I nodded, proud of myself for coming up with it off the top of my buzzing head.

"A tongue extender. You actually said 'a tongue extender.'"

"Prosthetics. Like in the movies."

"Please, elaborate. I'm curious. How, exactly, would a tongue extender work?"

I shrugged. "How would I know? I don't work in the entertainment industry. People make a lot of money to—"

"Craft tongue extenders for members of private clubs?"

"Hey, I can't explain why people do what they do."

Sky shook his head. "And you call *me* a crazy person. Then how about the—"

"Descendants of Astronauts?" I interrupted.

"*Asterion.*"

"Two big dudes who spend way too much time at the gym." My words felt thin, but they toppled out faster as Sky swung the car onto my street. I wanted to make my point before the night was over—to him or myself, I wasn't sure. "Bouncers with roid rage. They were crazy with it. They were . . ." I paused, noticing the way his lips were twitching up at the corners. "What?"

Sky pulled my car into the driveway and killed the engine. He flicked off the headlights, unhooked his seat belt, and shifted in his seat to face me. "You honestly don't believe Misty is a succubus," he said. It wasn't a question; it was an accusation. "Even though you used the word your-self."

I nodded. "Correct. It was the vodka talking."

He edged toward me, his green eyes roving over my face. With the car turned off, the night felt quiet and thick and dark around us. My fingers twitched against each other, and I realized they wanted to sink into Sky's messy blond hair and slide down the back of his neck . . .

I shoved both hands under my thighs.

"You think she was just a tall woman," he went on. "A tall woman in a fetish club."

I swallowed. "Yes."

"Nothing at all magic or supernatural about her, right?"

"You have a point?" I asked in a hollow voice, my eyes searching his.

Sky leaned in and touched his forehead lightly to mine. Despite everything we'd done that night, he smelled like clean laundry. A warm blanket. Something I wanted to wrap myself up in. I couldn't move, could barely breathe. I closed my eyes. He slid his head to the side, still hardly touching me, letting the side of his face drift against my own. His cheek—only a little rough—moved gently next to mine. His breath was warm in my hair. I felt his lips touch my earlobe and then skim upward, and I knew he had to be hearing my heart because it was pounding so loudly.

"I'm going to ask you something," he whispered.

"Yes." I wasn't sure if I was giving him permission to ask the question or giving him an answer for any question he might pose. His hand slid down my bare arm and onto my torso, stopping at my waist, right under where my shirt was still knotted up to the side. His thumb moved in small circles against my skin, and a shiver went through me.

"If you don't think Misty is a succubus, then why did you kiss me?"

I heard a *click.* He had unsnapped my seat belt. I jerked back against the car door and glared at him. "What?"

"Either you know Misty is a succubus and you were saving me from her spell, or you still don't believe it and you just wanted to kiss me." Sky arched his eyebrows. "Which is it?"

"I . . ."

"You can't have it both ways," said Sky.

I glared at him. And then, because I didn't have an answer, I got out, slammed the door (of my own car, I might add), and stalked up the driveway.

Behind me, I heard the driver's side door open and close. I listened to Sky's footsteps disappear into the night.

NINETEEN

There was still no electricity on the home front, obviously. Even though I was dying to tear my father's house apart for more clues about Rosemary-Who-Might-Be-My-Sister—and maybe even look up some of his old lectures on descendants of Asterion—it would all have to wait for sunlight. Besides, I was exhausted. I trudged up to my apartment and dropped fully clothed onto the futon.

I fell into a fractured, restless sleep, one where I found myself reliving the same incident over and over again. I was crouched on concrete with danger barreling toward me. Over and over, I jerked awake before the moment of impact. Over and over, the memory of how I'd been saved slipped away.

WEDNESDAY MORNING, WHEN I finally staggered out of bed, there weren't enough minutes left to take a shower or eat breakfast. I made a mental note to rethink the tradition of driving Norbert to school. As I pulled on the closest items of (reasonably) clean clothing—a black denim skirt and a T-shirt screen printed with the word FIGHT—I contemplated playing hooky. Maybe even dropping out. After all, I was already living the life of an adult. What more could I possibly gain or learn while being imprisoned five days a week with a bunch of kids whose biggest concern was prom?

Then again, the life I was living wasn't exactly the norm. Either for a teenager *or* an adult. And I did want more from real adulthood than a continued existence as a fake paranormal investigator. I assumed I would need a diploma in order to forge ahead in a different field, but I didn't know what that different field might look like. What did I want to be when I grew up? What would I be qualified to do? Clearly, not family therapy . . .

WHILE SLALOMING THROUGH TRAFFIC, I gave Norbert a rushed and garbled summary of the previous day's events. I glossed over the paranormal portion, as well as the vodka part of the vodka cranberries. I also didn't mention the part where I kissed Sky. I pretty much kept to the horror: getting chased by oversize thugs. In return, my cousin gave me a name.

"Dade Lawson."

"Who?"

"Remember? That janitor from Valley College who wanted us to put a hex on the trig professor."

"Right, that guy." I swerved around a garbage truck and gunned through a yellow light. "We convinced him to go with the Egyptian locust plague instead."

"Yeah. We put a dozen cockroaches in the professor's desk."

I nodded. "Lawson thought he didn't get his money's worth."

"Even though we gave him a partial refund," said Norbert.

I thought for a moment as I shifted lanes again. Dade Lawson, as I remembered, was basically a more human version of my attackers the previous night: a gym rat who also happened to believe in black magic. "Nah. I don't think he sent the obituary. He wasn't smart enough to come up with something like that. Anyone else?"

"Hey, can you stop zigzagging?" Norbert scrolled on his phone. "One more. Here it is. Marion Blewitt."

"Who?" Good thing I had Norbert around to keep track of details.

"That old lady in Chatsworth who was convinced her cat was Cleopatra reincarnated."

I grimaced. "And then Cat-Cleo got run over by a soccer mom in a minivan." I jammed into a parking space by the school. "We had nothing to do with that." I wondered if Marion Blewitt was her real name. I suppose I should have wondered that at the time of her case.

"Still, not a satisfied customer," Norbert said. He hopped out and slammed the door just as the bell rang from inside the school. Then he was off like a sprinter.

I followed, feeling queasy and hot. Coming here was a mistake.

Geometry class started with a discussion of proofs. Considering that my days were already spent trying to prove things that couldn't possibly exist, it was stupid that I had to waste an hour of my time explaining why Triangle A was congruent with Triangle B. Especially when the answer apparently had to involve a bunch of memorized theorems and postulates instead of the simple answer I tried to provide when called on.

"They're just the same." I slumped further into my chair.

"But *why*?" asked Mrs. Keplin.

"Because they look the same."

"That's not enough," said Mrs. Keplin. "I need a theorem."

"How about the theorem of 'Duh'?"

Some classmates giggled. Some glared. Mrs. Keplin shook her head and scribbled something in her notebook.

Great. Another year, another class participation grade gone to hell.

AT LUNCHTIME, I BOUGHT a wilted salad and ate it on the hood of my car, mentally going over everything I knew about Corabelle's case. Given what had happened in Little Tokyo, I needed to explore all possibilities. No matter whether Misty *was* a succubus or *believed* she was a succubus (maybe the difference was unimportant) or was just a crazy fetish queen, I had to take a good look at her connection to Todd Harmon.

When I finished my salad, I jotted down two sets of notes: one that any real investigator would use and one that operated strictly in Lunatic Land. One of the two would lead to Todd Harmon. At least, I hoped so.

A phone search on (sigh!) succubi led me to several websites, including a few that featured articles by my father (sigh again). There was conflicting information about the details, but the general definition was pretty much the same across the board: a succubus was a lady demon who fed off human men.

Exactly what Sky had said.

Maybe he knew what he was talking about. Or maybe he'd just been to these websites too, the difference being he had been a believer going in.

I tried to look at things objectively. If I could buy the existence of succubi (still a leap), then I could also theoretically buy the idea that, in order to live, they required different sustenance than what normal humans needed. If, as these sites claimed, that sustenance was male "life force"—a euphemism for something completely disgusting—then feeding off human men kept succubi alive and made them stronger.

Okay, I could wrap my head around that if it weren't for this one thing: getting certain males to have sex is hardly a difficult task. Especially if you're a hot succubus with the ability to turn dudes to Jell-O with a gaze. Considering the number of horny teenaged boys at my school alone, it seemed like a succubus could screw her way to the top of the food chain in a single afternoon. If succubi existed, why weren't they ruling the world?

I was about to begin a search on "history of demons" when the bell rang. Lunch was over. I had already sent several texts to Norbert with no answer, so I'd finally fired off one to Sky, too. In return, I'd gotten nothing.

Silence from my cousin and silence from my . . . whatever he was.

WHEN I GOT TO Greek Mythology, the room had been rearranged so all the chairs were facing inward in a big circle. I sat down between two empty seats and dropped my backpack onto one of them to save it for Sky. It wasn't that I *wanted* to be near him; it was that I had some thoughts about Todd Harmon that warranted discussion.

At least, that was the angle I would go with.

If he ever showed up.

After Mr. Lowe sauntered into the classroom and closed the door, and Sky still hadn't arrived, I started to get pissed. I hadn't seen or heard from him all day. Sure, I had contemplated bailing on school myself, but I hadn't actually done it.

I watched Mr. Lowe lift a plastic basket off his desk and drop it onto the desk in front of the seat I'd saved. "You can put your index cards in here."

Damn it. I had forgotten all about that dumb homework assignment.

I raised my hand and waited for Mr. Lowe to nod at me. "I have to powder my nose," I told him, using the code every male teacher in every high school knows. This is the one thing that's awesome about menstruation: guy teachers will never—and I mean *never*—stop you from going to the bathroom.

Moments later, I was standing by a dirty sink, skimming a finger over my phone. My connection wasn't great, but I was able to pull up a website dedicated to characters from Greek mythology. It was easy to find a good one: Persephone. Daughter of Zeus and the Queen of the Underworld. She sounded sufficiently badass to me.

I pulled out my index card and scribbled her name on it. When I got back to class, I shoved it into the basket among the others while Mr. Lowe's back was turned to the whiteboard.

Whew.

Even better, we were instructed to spend the next twenty minutes of class reading while Mr. Lowe looked over the cards. Translation: quality phone time, hidden by my textbook. I wasn't sure what my next move should be on the case, so I searched "fake obituary" on the off chance it was a *thing* and not a specific threat aimed at me. My heart sank. The only results were about a white-collar criminal in Florida who was scamming life insurance companies.

Just as troubling: still no Sky by the time Mr. Lowe told us he was ready to guess who had chosen which character.

"As I've only met some of you this week, I'm taking chances," he announced. "Of course, there are those whose reputations precede them."

Mr. Lowe struck out on his first guess but then nailed two in a row.

Peter Penn—a dude who wore enough black eyeliner to make me look like a ray of sunshine—was Thanatos, the Demon Personification of Death. Our resident hottie, Angel Ortega, was an easy one as Aphrodite: the Goddess of Love, Beauty, and Pleasure. When Mr. Lowe said her name, Angel fluttered her eyelashes. Of course she did.

From across the circle, Lauren-or-Laurel accidentally made eye contact with me. She flushed and looked down, like she'd done something wrong. I wondered if there was a Herald of the Hopelessly Damaged in the stack.

Mr. Lowe looked at the next card and nodded. "Perse-phone," he told us, and then paused, letting his gaze drift around the room from person to person.

I waited to hear about Persephone's badassery. I didn't know how much this assignment was worth, but I hoped turning in someone so obviously suited for me meant I'd start off the year with a decent grade.

"This student made a brave choice," said Mr. Lowe. "Persephone was a beautiful and warm-hearted girl until Death wrenched her away from her mother."

Wait—what?!

"Persephone was kidnapped by Hades and dragged down to be his bride in the Underworld," said Mr. Lowe. "She sealed her fate by eating a pomegranate. Nobody can eat the food of the dead and return to the world of the living. Some see her as the Queen of the Damned. Others see her as a cautionary tale."

That was more like it.

"But astute scholars know her for who she really was. Someone forced to leave home too soon." His voice soft-ened. "A child missing her mother."

No, no, no, no, no . . .

"A girl in pain." I was frozen, horrified as Mr. Lowe's compassionate eyes settled upon mine. "Persephone?"

Heat burned up my throat, stopping my breath and quick-ening my pulse. I would rather have been back in that alley. I would rather have been anywhere but there in that class-room for everyone to see me for what I truly was.

Scared.

Tragic.

A victim.

I had no idea what I was going to say, but I opened my mouth—and then closed it.

Lauren-or-Laurel had her hand raised.

"It was me," she said in her wispy voice. "I'm Persephone."

Mr. Lowe turned to her, confused. "You're Persephone? Are you sure?"

She nodded, her mouth set in a resolute line. "I'm sure."

Mr. Lowe glanced back at me. "Why did you choose Persephone?" he asked her.

She swallowed, and her answer sounded more like a question. "I really like pomegranates?"

As the class burst into laughter, I grabbed my backpack and lurched to my feet. "I'm sorry, I have a headache," I said before charging for the door. Mr. Lowe didn't try to stop me, but I felt his and Lauren-or-Laurel's eyes on me the entire way.

ALTHOUGH I SLUNK AROUND the halls, ducking into bathrooms and janitor's closets any time a teacher came near, I ended up running into somebody after the bell rang. Not Sky (who'd apparently ditched) and not Norbert (who had a free study period).

No, it was Corabelle who fell into step beside me.

"How far have you gotten on my case?" she asked. She didn't sound happy.

"Far. Really far."

"Do you know where Todd is?" she demanded.

"Not that far."

Corabelle grabbed my arm and pulled me to a halt.

"Stop screwing around. You're supposed to be working for me, remember? Instead all you've done is waste my money and my time."

"Not true," I snapped, yanking my arm away. "I've made a lot of progress. Investigations take time."

"I don't *have* time. I'm falling apart."

I took a good look at her. It was true; Corabelle didn't look so hot. Her usual perfect blonde hair was lank, falling in greasy strands to her shoulders. Her face was shiny, and she had a small cluster of pimples along her left jawline. There were light purple smudges under her eyes. Her lips were even more chapped than they had been.

"Where's Sky?" she asked, glaring at me.

"I'm not his keeper."

"Aren't you his partner?"

"According to him. But you hired *me*. Why? Do you need something to play with while your boyfriend's out of the picture?" I knew I probably shouldn't have said it, but this entire day was starting to piss me off.

"I don't care that Sky wants me. He can get in line. I want my *own* boyfriend back." Her chapped lips trembled. "When I hired *you*, I was under the impression that you would be able to find Todd Harmon, the boy I love. Of course, I was also under the impression that Umbra Investigations was something a little more legit than the high school freak show no one wants to sit next to."

I froze, staring back at her. Feeling my fingers clench into fists. It would have been the easiest thing in the world to punch her right in the face. But then . . .

Then.

She'd tell everyone the truth. She'd take away my case. I'd be left with no alibi, no money, nothing. I wouldn't have a secret identity. I wouldn't have *anything*. I really *would* be the freak show everyone avoids. The one with no electricity. The one with no parents. The one who might have a date with death in six months.

And so, although it required everything in my power to do it, I took a deep breath. I relaxed my fingers. "I'm sorry," I said, as sincerely as I could manage. "Give me the weekend."

"Tell me one good reason why I should."

"Here are two." I shot her a hard smile. "One, the police can't find Todd. Two, I can."

God, I hoped that was true.

Corabelle took a step backward, her eyes still locked on mine. "Friday," she said. "Find him by Friday, or I get my money back and tell the cops myself. And then I let everyone at school know who you really are."

She turned and stormed away, her long ponytail swinging behind her. Her face may have taken a nose dive, but she clearly hadn't lost any beauty in her ass; a handful of guys turned to stare longingly at it until she disappeared around the corner. I was furious at them, at their dumb boy desire for a pretty, shitty girl. I was furious at Corabelle for being that girl. Worse, I was furious at myself. Out of the awful things Corabelle had said, the one that stung the most was the one about Sky wanting her. She was so sure of it, so nonchalant.

It was all that pent-up fury that ended up getting me thrown in detention.

TWENTY

Any other day, I would have walked right past three jocks making fun of a girl whose books had fallen out of her locker. Any other day, I wouldn't have noticed how one of the jocks kicked the books so that when the girl bent over to get them, another could grab her by the hips and mime banging her from behind. Any other day, it wouldn't have mattered that the girl was Lauren-or-Laurel, or that she was crying.

It wasn't any other day.

I tapped the mime banger on the shoulder. When he turned around, I slammed my fist into his nose.

He went down hard and spat something from the floor that was impossible to understand. Ignoring him, I faced his two friends. One had gone silent, but the other—the bigger, book-kicking one—took a step in my direction. I jerked my hand up in front of his face. "See, no bruising. It's all in the curvature of the swing. You keep your thumb on the outside and it doesn't break. All the things I will do to you, they won't hurt me at all. You, on the other hand . . ."

"You're full of shit," he said. But his voice wavered.

"That's what Mario Amello thought. Ask him how his balls were after our last interaction." I took a step closer. "Or ask around about the razors I keep on my person at all times."

"You don't have a razor. I don't *see* a razor."

"They're hidden." I stepped right up to him, dropping my voice. "One is in my boot. One is in my hair." I saw him glance up at the messy knot atop my head. "And the other one," I whispered, "is somewhere very, very secret. If you ever again even *look* like you're going to touch me"—I glanced at Lauren-or-Laurel, who was trying to melt into the lockers—"or her, or *any* other girl, I will introduce all three razors to you."

He backed away, his face frozen in a look of fear, disgust, or confusion—or all three. Behind him, the quiet jock pulled the other one up from the floor. "Come on," he said. They limped off. And just like that, every trace of the three was gone. Except for some tearstains on the floor.

I picked up Lauren-or-Laurel's books and handed them to her. Her gaze rose to the top of my head, and I offered a grim smile. "I don't really have a razor hidden in my hair."

She nodded, her eyes wide.

"I don't have razors hidden anywhere else either, so try to stay out of trouble," I told her.

I had started down the hallway when I heard her voice behind me. "Wait. Why did you do that?"

I turned. "Who did you really pick for mythology?"

"Artemis."

Of course I wasn't familiar.

"She likes children and nature," Lauren-or-Laurel explained. "And she's a virgin."

"You wanted to advertise that?" I asked. No reason to mention that I was sailing in the same sea of celibacy.

Lauren-or-Laurel shrugged. "It's not like anyone would be surprised. Besides, Artemis is cooler than she seems. She's the goddess of the hunt."

"So why didn't you tell Mr. Lowe you were Artemis?"

"Because." She paused, as if considering the answer before she gave it. "Because when I saw your face, you looked the way I feel all the time. Scared."

"There you go," I said. "I kicked that cretin's ass because of Persephone."

The tiniest smile twitched at the corners of her mouth. "Thanks."

"Can I ask you something? What's your name?"

The smile broadened, lighting up her whole face. "It's Laura."

I'd been double wrong this whole time. I smiled back, feeling almost like a normal girl . . . until Principal Vander rounded the corner and handed me a detention slip.

Those stupid jocks.

TWENTY-ONE

The only exciting thing that happened in detention was a reminder text from Corabelle:

Find Todd by Fri or Im telling every1 abot Umbra

Besides that, the passage of time was marked only by me and the other degenerates staring at each other in resentful silence.

I was almost to my car when my phone rang.

"Where are you?" Sky asked the minute I answered.

"Where are *you*? I've been trying to find you all day!"

"See, that's what I like to hear." His voice went soft, and so did my insides. "But we're on a case, so we should probably stick to the topic at hand. Meet me at Norbert's."

"Wait, why are you at . . ."

But I was talking to myself. Sky had already hung up.

OF COURSE AUNT AGGIE and Uncle Edmund were at home, and of course they couldn't have been happier to see me on their doorstep. Before I could say hello, I got swooped into one of my aunt's signature angel-love hugs while my uncle clapped me on the shoulder with his heavy hand.

"There's a boy downstairs with Norbert," Uncle Edmund told me. "Nice manners. Good teeth. You should check him out."

I pulled away from Aggie's tight embrace. "How many hands tall is he?"

My uncle didn't even begin to understand the sarcasm of my horse analogy. "Seventeen, maybe. Or eighteen. What's the horse-to-metric ratio again?"

"I'll take a look, Uncle Edmund."

"Good thinking, Jillian. You do that."

"Do you want lemonade?" Aunt Aggie didn't wait for me to answer. "Go on. I'll bring it in."

I headed down the thinly carpeted stairs stained with the residue of someone else's life.

My aunt and uncle had rented the house two years earlier when they moved back in a hurry so that—unlike my useless father—they could help with Mom. Since I had refused to live with them, and since Dad had supported my decision in absentia from wherever he was in the Middle East or the Himalayas or the Amazon at the time, Aggie and Edmund had leased the closest place they could find: a small ranch house that had peaked in the eighties. Lots of peach and turquoise wallpaper. The basement was a plus, unusual because most California houses don't have them. Earthquakes.

As I descended, my cousin's class photos descended the wall alongside me, a trip back in time. By the time I reached the bottom step, a chubby five-year-old beamed out at me. That was the Norbert I remembered from our last normal family vacation: a trip to Pilot, North Carolina, where Norbert's family used to live. Back when my family could still pass for normal.

The musty basement smell was comforting in its familiarity. As was the wood paneling. Preexisting decor aside, my aunt and uncle had furnished the room in a way that they believed to be inviting for Norbert's potential teenaged guests. Rickety Ping-Pong table. Dorm-size refrigerator filled with sodas. Some sort of video-game console hooked up to an ancient, bulbous television set.

Norbert and Sky had pulled the room's two faux-suede, oversized beanbags together. Both were tapping away on their laptops. They barely looked up when I walked in, but Sky scooted over and patted his beanbag.

"Share with me."

I was torn but curious, and—let's be honest—the desire to be close to him won out. I plopped down on the cushion. "You better have something good."

"We do," Sky told me. "Your cousin is amazing."

Norbert gave a modest shrug from the other beanbag. "It's a gift."

"We're hoping to hear back from your dad, but he hasn't—"

"Wait, what?" I grabbed Sky's arm.

Norbert gave Sky a sour look. "Dude."

"Dude what?" Sky asked innocently.

"What's going on?" I threw out my arms, giving them both a whap. "Why are you talking to my father?"

"Don't freak out," said Norbert. "I emailed Uncle Lewis.

I asked for everything he's got on succubi." He ignored my grunt of disapproval. "He hasn't written back yet, but I'm hoping he'll give us something more than what we can find online."

"Whatever." I couldn't be gracious about anything associated with Dad. I turned to Sky's computer. "So what did you come up with?"

His screen was open to a real estate website. "Misty said her lair is in Leimert Park, so we've been looking at locations there."

"Succubi have very specific housing requirements," chimed in Norbert.

"Such as?"

"Obviously, they can't have too many windows," said Sky. "And they need some distance from their neighbors."

"Which rules out most of Los Angeles," I said.

"Exactly," Norbert told me. "But there are plenty of places with cinder block walls around the property, so we're trying to focus on those. Also, succubi need natural gas heating and easy access to mass transit."

"Wait, what?"

"Succubi don't drive," Sky explained.

"Why?"

Sky looked thoughtful. "Honestly, I don't know. But my research says they don't, so it's part of the equation."

I looked at a map on his screen. "That doesn't make any sense. If Misty took the Metro into the Valley that day, she would have had to get back to the station in sunlight. Wouldn't that be a problem?"

"Not if she had a driver."

"A driver," I repeated.

Norbert spun his computer around to face me. "That's another part of the equation. We're cross-checking information on privately owned hearses."

"Hearses! Even for a fictional succubus, doesn't that seem a little bit cliché?"

"Maybe," said Norbert. "But if you were a sun-hating man sucker, trust me: a carrier of death would be the way to go."

My cousin was loving this. I was almost happy for him.

Sky nudged my leg with his own. "Look. We narrowed it down."

I peered at a list of six addresses. Again, I weighed all the different types of crazy in my head. It came down to what we already knew: Todd Harmon was missing, and this Misty chick was involved. No matter what she was—succubus or sicko—getting a look at her home base might give us a clue as to Todd's whereabouts. Besides, the clock was ticking. The high school rumor mill didn't care what sort of contract Corabelle had signed. If she told everyone the truth—that I was Umbra Investigations (and terrible at my job)—what little life I had was over.

I checked my watch. Almost five. Even with no traffic, driving to Leimert Park would take us close to an hour. And in Los Angeles, "no traffic" was every bit as fictional as "paranormal investigation."

"Let's go," I said.

GETTING OUT OF THE house took longer than I would have liked. First, the printer jammed while printing out the list of addresses. Then Norbert couldn't find one of his favorite boots. Right when it looked like we were on the brink of escape, we were waylaid by Aunt Aggie and her lemonade. Then Sky felt compelled to butter her up with praise for the handmade beverage.

I was irritated at first, but I didn't see his end game coming. Aggie didn't blink an eye when he told her that we were taking Norbert out "to look at the stars for astronomy class."

Are you kidding? Does any high school even offer astronomy?

We still might have made reasonable time had it not been rush hour and had we not encountered an ill-timed light summer mist. Rain happens so rarely in Southern California that when it does, people are astounded. Water from the skies! Everyone forgets how to drive. By the time I had fought my way down the 405 and slid into a space in a big, empty parking lot, the sun was on its way down.

Beneath the deepening shade of a sycamore tree at the edge of the lot, I ripped Norbert's printout into three pieces, one for each of us.

"Here's the deal," I said with a stern look at my cousin. "This is a fact-finding mission, and that is *it*. Two addresses each, all within walking distance from here. Use the GPS on your phone and take pictures. If there's a trash bin and you can get a quickie shot of what's inside, awesome. Same with mailboxes. Small talk with neighbors is fine, but don't get caught snooping, and don't enter any buildings. Everyone clear?"

Sky gave me a mock salute. "Aye, aye."

"Right here," I told them both. "By eight o'clock."

"Copy that." Norbert checked the blue lights on his watch. "Twenty hundred hours, this location." He performed a less ironic version of Sky's salute before dashing off. Sky and I watched him arrive at the corner of Forty-Third and Degnan and stop to look both ways. He actually hopped up and down while he waited for a car to pass. This *was* making him happy. You had to give it to the kid. He had enthusiasm for miles.

I was starting to enter the first of the addresses into my phone's GPS when Sky's hand covered my own.

"Hey," he said. "I'm sorry about last night."

I stopped typing but had to take a split second to compose myself before looking up into his eyes. "For ripping up my favorite Hater shirt? It's fine. Probably looks better with a wide neck."

Sky's fingers lingered. "That's not what I'm talking about."

"Oh, that thing where you got me drunk? And fed me your own blood? That's cool too. First time for everything and all that."

He lifted my hand away from the phone. "Be real with me. Just for a second, and then you can go back to . . . the way you are."

I swallowed. I was tempted to be pissed. But he was right. I was . . . the way I was. I didn't know how to be anything else. When I didn't speak, he lowered our hands, entwining his fingers with mine so I couldn't pull away. He took a step closer. "I shouldn't have teased you. You saved me."

"You dropped a piano on a guy for me," I said. "I think we're even."

"I don't think so," said Sky. "I think I owe you something."

"Gas money?"

He shook his head, flashing that white, bright grin. My pulse quickened. All I could think was, *Good teeth.* Uncle Edmund was right.

"I owe you a kiss."

It had stopped raining, but the air was still thick and damp.

I shook my head. "I didn't ask to cash in on that debt." I meant it to be snarky, but it came out in a whisper.

Sky's left hand grazed my hip before sliding around me and up my back. "One good kiss deserves another," he said. He stopped smiling. His voice wasn't jokey anymore either. Instead it was low and soft, and his eyes were shining and focused on mine. He lowered his head toward me, and I felt the last shreds of my prideful resistance give up the ghost.

"I don't think that's how the phrase goes," I murmured, tilting my face up, letting go, finally ready to succumb like I had in the dark terror of that succubus nightclub . . .

. . . and then we were kissing. Moving against each other. Hands and arms. Skin. I didn't plan to touch his messy blond hair, but suddenly my fingers were twining through it, trying to bring him even closer to me. I was melting. I was drowning. I was spinning. My whole being was wide open, allowing me—for once—to just be. Just. Be.

Just.

Be.

I'm not sure what tore me out of that place, but even as I felt his fingers tighten on my waist, something nagged at me. Something tickled my brain, and Sky's kisses couldn't make me ignore it.

I pulled away, trying to catch my breath. "Wait."

Sky looked down at me, bewildered. He drew me closer, his thumbs still tracing figure eights against my hips, and all I wanted was to let him do it.

But I didn't.

I set my hand flat against his chest. I pushed him away.

"Why?" he asked.

"That's my question too." I paused to give my pulse a chance to slow down. "Why?"

Sky's eyebrows scrunched up in the middle. "I'm confused."

"So am I." I stepped back, putting another foot of distance between us. It wasn't much, but the space helped me regain my sanity. "Why me?"

"What are you talking about?"

"You could have your pick of girls," I told him. "Prettier ones. More normal ones. Blonder ones."

"Prettier, no. More blonde and normal, maybe . . ."

I ignored both compliment and insult and asked the question that had been haunting me all along. "Is it just because I'm Lewis Cade's daughter?"

Something—an emotion I couldn't identify, but had seen before—flashed over Sky's face, and his grin fell away. Neither of us moved. But there was more distance between us now. I didn't have the capacity to explain that I had never felt this way before, that no guy had ever kissed me in a way that made me lose my breath and my mind. I couldn't explain that I didn't even like *myself* all that much, and so it made no sense to me whatsoever that he might. I definitely couldn't tell him that Corabelle knew that he wanted her.

"Jillian." He said my name in a whisper. "In all of this, have I ever hurt you?" He didn't wait for me to answer. "No. I wouldn't hurt you. I would never hurt you. All I want to do is protect you. That's why . . . you have to believe me when I tell you it's fate."

I stared at him, the ache in my throat making it hard to speak. "I believe that you think it's fate, but there's no such thing."

"Jillian, trust me—"

"I don't." It came out of my mouth like a bullet. I watched the hurt flash over his face.

"That's because you don't know me," he said.

"Exactly. If you really want to protect me, then help me. We're supposed to be getting photos, not making out in public like horny teenagers." Even as I said it, I knew how he would respond.

"We *are* horny teenagers."

"Speak for yourself. This thing between us—"

"This connection."

"This whatever-it-is, we put it on hold until we find Todd Harmon. It's a deal I made with myself, and you have to respect it."

For a moment, Sky seemed to consider. Then, like it had never been gone, that cocky half smile was back. "Motivation. I like it." He reached into his pocket and pulled out the scrap of paper with his two addresses on it. "See you back here."

"Soon," I said.

"Very soon."

We headed in opposite directions.

One thing I *did* learn from my father: never look back (even the Bible says you could turn into a pillar of salt). Maybe defying Dad was what compelled me to do it. That's how I saw Sky slow to a standstill beside the last sycamore tree in the parking lot. I wanted to run back and fling my arms around him.

Instead, I waited. I watched as his shoulders slumped. I watched as he scuffed at the sidewalk with a dirty tennis shoe. And I jumped when he slammed his hand into the rough bark of the tree.

Then I whirled around and ran.

Not because I didn't want Sky to know I'd seen him. Not because I had no idea how to handle someone else's pain or rage or confusion. It was because running away was the one thing that came naturally to me.

Besides, I had a job to do.

TWENTY-TWO

I checked my scrap of paper and decided to head to the address on Eleventh Avenue. It was furthest away; I'd go there first and work my way back. I crossed Creed to avoid a group of older teenagers swarming around the hood of a parked car blasting rap. The heavy *thud-thud* of the bass followed me as I skirted a man selling frozen mango slices out of a pushcart. Then I took a left on Eleventh.

At first glance, the block wasn't promising. Lawns were patchy and dry, and they fronted what appeared to be older homes that had been cut up into apartment buildings. Halfway up the block, a blue recycling bin was tipped over on the sidewalk, its contents of empty Old Milwaukee and King Cobra bottles strewn everywhere.

Granted, I didn't really know Misty-the-Potential-Succubus. But thus far this wasn't looking like a place she would call home.

At least, that's what I thought before I saw the limousine.

In typical limousine fashion, it was long and sleek and

black. In less typical fashion, it was hanging out on crappy-ass Eleventh Avenue in Leimert Park, idling at the curb in front of the second to the last building on my side of the street . . . the building I was supposed to check out.

I felt my steps slow as thoughts began to turn in my brain. First and foremost: If Misty herself stepped out of that limousine, what would I do if she saw me? After all, the last time we'd laid eyes on each other, I'd roofied her with Sky's blood before sucking his face, and then she'd sent her crazed bodyguards after me. "Hey, wassup?" hardly seemed like the way to go.

I was still a house away when the back passenger window slid noiselessly down and an arm extended from the limo. A dark, walnut-skinned arm with defined biceps. And a hand holding a black flower.

I froze and slid my phone from the back pocket of my jeans, but it slipped from my clammy fingers and dropped onto the sidewalk. There was a cracking sound when it landed. As I squatted to grab it, I saw the splintered spider web across the screen.

Shit.

I skimmed my finger over the now-shattered glass. It still worked . . . at least enough for me to open my camera app and point the lens at the limo. On the broken screen, I saw the brown biceps of that arm bulge and glisten in the dimming sunlight and then darken as a shadow fell over it.

Something else was emerging from the window.

I tried to make myself small—as if I had a prayer of going invisible, crouching there on the sidewalk—and watched as the thing surged from the window, right above that muscled arm. The thing was a shaved head with a neat goatee and a pair of mirrored sunglasses.

"Speed it up, Frannie!" the head barked. "We're gonna lose our table."

"Chill, douchebag."

I whipped my gaze to the right. A woman was tottering out atop a fire-red pair of stilettos. Their color exactly matched her miniskirt and halter top and lipstick and hair.

She looked like an extremely tall, skinny, busty tomato.

"Hey, I bought you a fuckin' rose!" Baldy shouted.

The tomato lady snorted. "It's black. What the hell is a black rose?"

"It's not black. It's deep red. It's called Night Owl, and it's expensive as hell."

"That's screwed up."

"That's love, bitch!"

The tomato woman reached the limo and planted a kiss right on the guy's mouth. "I love you too, baby."

She climbed inside. I smiled at the limo as it glided away from the curb. Here were people who seemed way stranger than me but nonetheless managed to have successful relationships.

I really needed to figure some things out.

To cover my bases, I kept heading north on the sidewalk so I could pass the building the woman had exited. I got a couple photos of it on my phone and peered inside the trash bin but didn't see anything suspicious. Of course, I wasn't entirely sure what I was looking for.

The sun was no longer visible, but the streetlights hadn't

yet come to life. Maybe they were on timers. Or just for show. Or broken.

I turned left at the end of the block and left again. This street—Edgehill—was shadier than the other. Huge sycamores lined both sides, their dense branches spread out over me. In front of the first house I passed, a skinny girl about my age squatted on an upside-down bucket, picking at her fingernails. She looked up as I walked by.

"You here for blow?" she asked.

"No," I told her. "Something else. But thank you."

We nodded at each other. I continued on. My second destination was a two-story house halfway down the block. The bottom floor was made out of stucco. The top appeared to be wood that had been painted peach. A faded Christmas wreath hung on the front door. I had a hard time believing Misty would decorate for the birthday of the baby Jesus, but one never knew. Maybe she was trying to pass for normal with her neighbors. Maybe the wreath had already been there when she moved in and ate the previous occupant. After all, it was slightly more reasonable to think that she was a cannibal than a succubus . . .

I took a picture from the sidewalk. There were no lights on in the house, so either no one was home, or whoever lived there was hanging out in the dark. I was about to leave when I saw something: a torn piece of paper on the house's cracked walkway. I glanced around. The block was deserted aside from the girl on her bucket, and from where I was standing, she was nothing more than a dim, shadowed outline. I was alone.

I darted up the pavement, snatched the paper, and was

back on the sidewalk within a matter of seconds. Shoving the scrap into my pocket, I sprinted to the end of the block—which put me again at Creed, across from the big empty parking lot, and also put me significantly out of breath.

I scooted into a streetlamp's pool of light and yanked out the scrap. It was a half page of newspaper, ragged along one edge where it had been ripped away. As I'd hoped (or maybe feared?), now that I had it in my hand, I could see that it was exactly what it had looked like.

The obituary section.

I touched the paper, feeling its litho-or-web-fed-or-whatever-Eddie-said roughness under my fingertips, and held it up so my shadow wasn't blocking the light from the streetlamp falling onto it. A rectangular section had been ripped out of the top center of the page. The upper edge had been ripped away with it, including the part where the newspaper's date would have been.

I really wished I had my obituary—my fake, creepy obituary—with me so I could compare the two pieces.

It could have been a coincidence. But I knew it wasn't. It was just another thing that defied explanation. These days, there were so many. Todd Harmon's disappearance. Misty's tongue. My sister's name on my future obituary.

Sky.

Nothing made sense anymore.

I folded the paper twice.

And then I paused. And opened it. And turned it over.

On the other side was an advertisement: a full-page spread for Target, hawking the joys of purchasing back-to-school supplies, featuring a cute girl in a denim jumper and glasses (because spectacles equal scholastic achievement; thanks, marketing geniuses!). Someone had used a red pen to circle various items. Post-it notes for the low, low price of $1.99 had been circled . . . and then crossed out.

Apparently the red pen's owner thought he or she could do better.

Around the empty portion—the part that had been ripped out—parts of red lines were still visible. The owner of this paper was going to save fifty cents on rounded scissors or maybe mechanical pencils. I crumpled it, shoving it into my pocket. This piece of paper wasn't about the obituaries after all. It didn't have a damn thing to do with me, or with the Todd Harmon case.

It was a reminder that there *were* no coincidences. Everything had to have an explanation.

That's when my phone rang.

I nearly jumped out of my skin, of course. Naturally my next response was to hope it was Sky calling. But no such luck. The letters on my screen spelled the name Ernie Stuart. Ha! That *was* a coincidence. Or not. I almost didn't answer, but curiosity won out. "Hey, Ernie."

"Hello, this is Ernie Stuart. Can I talk to—" He paused. "You kids and your caller ID. How are you, honey?"

"I'm great, Ernie. What's going on?"

"Thought you'd want to know my buddy got back to me."

I squinted across Creed to see if Sky or Norbert was back yet. It was too dark to tell. "Oh yeah?" I said into the phone.

"He pulled a partial set of prints off your paper," Ernie told me. "Ran 'em through the California driver's license database. Turns out they belong to a kid."

That got my attention.

"Yup, I was right. Just a goofy joke. One of your classmates messing with you."

My heart lurched and then settled back into my chest. It felt tighter than it was supposed to be. Heavier. I knew what the name would be even before Ernie spoke it into my ear.

"Sky Ramsey."

TWENTY-THREE

My directions had been very specific. I had told everyone to meet back at the parking lot. Yet here I was, disobeying my own instructions. I couldn't do it.

Sky had lied.

No, it wasn't that small and simple. Our entire relationship—if you could call it that—was built on a heaping pile of bullshit. Sky had started with dishonesty and then shoveled lie after lie on top of it. From the moment I'd set eyes on him, it had been deception by omission. I'd forgiven all his earlier lies, because I was a liar too.

But this was different.

Sky was behind that fake obituary in my locker. He had confused me. Terrorized me. And he'd done it deliberately.

I couldn't risk being alone with him. I couldn't even see him. At least, not before I'd had a chance to think this over. Until I figured out his motive. I didn't know how I should react to him: with outrage, sorrow . . . *fear*? For now, if I saw him, I had to pretend I didn't know about his treachery. That was the only way I could get through this. Otherwise, it would hurt too much.

Norbert. Norbert was family. He was safety and sweetness and understanding. I had to find Norbert.

The problem was, I didn't have either of the addresses he was currently investigating. Stupid, stupid printout. I didn't know where either of them had gone. I pulled out my phone. I heaved a sigh of relief when the cracked screen allowed me to open my texting app. I shot Norbert a quick message:

where r u

While waiting for his answer, I scanned my brain. One of the addresses had been on a street that started with a *D*. Deadwood, maybe? Or Dunham? I checked the map on my phone and—*yes!*—there it was. Degnan Boulevard. I headed west on Forty-Third and turned right.

I walked the length of the block, giving a wide berth to a guy sleeping on the sidewalk. Across the street, there was a woman sitting on her front stoop. By the flickering light of her porch lantern, I could see that she was peeling carrots, letting the discarded strips fall onto the bottom step. Occasionally she gave her peeler a hard flick, and a piece would fly into the grass. She looked up and caught my stare. When she raised a hand in greeting, I did the same.

Still no sign of Norbert or Sky.

I turned left, then left again. South Norton Avenue was darker than the other streets, thanks to the low-hanging trees. I felt something touch my face and swatted at it, thinking it was a spider web, but it was a tiny raindrop. The mist was back, stickier and heavier than before.

Halfway down the deserted block, I heard a sound behind me, like shoes dragging across gravel. I whirled, but couldn't see a thing. Everything was inky stillness. I resumed my original path, seeing the streetlights of Forty-Third glowing faintly at the end of the block, my heart quickening in time with my feet.

I heard the hiss at the same time I felt coldness licking the skin of my left leg. I jerked in the direction of the street, pivoting. My boots sank into the grass. I tensed for an attack—

But there was no attacker. There was only a broken sprinkler head, spraying an arc across the sidewalk. Only water on my leg.

Between the not-succubus and Sky, I was coming unhinged.

I scraped my muddy boots as best as I could on the edge of the sidewalk, and then stepped toward the broken sprinkler. It had scared the crap out of me, so the least it could do was clean off my footwear. I held my right boot in the arc of water, hoping it would take off the worst of it . . .

When I saw something. A real something. It was there, in the mud beside the broken sprinkler head. It was fresh and it was clear.

The outline of the Millennium Falcon.

MY COUSIN HAD A *Battlestar Galactica* backpack. He had a cookie cutter in the shape of the starship *Enterprise,* and the outside of his bedroom closet was painted like a blue British police box. Norbert had no problem mixing metaphors or fictional universes. And although I worried that some future girl might be turned off by his Ewok sheets, maybe she too would admire his passion for all things classically geek.

Now looking down at the mud, I remembered the whole fuss when we were trying to leave his house: *the boots*. He'd had to find the right pair. They were necessary because they'd bring us good luck. *Star Wars* boots, with the outline of the Millennium Falcon engraved on the soles.

So very Norbert.

This particular Falcon imprint was pointed straight at the building looming over the patchy, muddy lawn. Beyond the first Falcon was another and then the blurred outline of a third.

Norbert had checked out this building.

Which was fine. We were *here* to check out buildings. But then I suddenly realized why this specific building looked different. It's because it was dark, darker than everything around it. And it wasn't because the lights were off. It was because the windows had been painted black.

I briefly considered texting Norbert or calling him again. Even more briefly, I considered calling Sky. Maybe there was a chance he wasn't actually an evil liar with a moral compass that stunk worse than hellfire. Perhaps he had good reason to scare me . . . and confuse me . . . and lie to me.

No. Sky was a terrible person—maybe even a sociopath—and I couldn't trust him at all. I couldn't go to him for help.

I was on my own.

Best to keep moving until I found Norbert. I crept along

the side of the building until I reached the back corner. I stepped just past it, to a nearby tree. Setting one hand against its rough trunk, I cast my phone around, using its dim light to hunt for anything that would clue me in to Norbert's whereabouts.

Nothing.

I aimed my phone at the building. I heard a gentle, rhythmic slapping sound but couldn't pinpoint the source. From back there, the building looked like it was probably a fourplex, with two apartments above and two below. On the bottom floor were two sliding doors leading onto two small patios made of cracked concrete. I peered into the gloominess between the patios and a wooden deck that stretched from one end of the second floor to the other.

My fingers and toes went numb.

The whole deck was covered with a giant piece of black tarp, as if to shield it from the sun. One side of the tarp was completely shredded. It looked like giant claws had ripped it from top to bottom. The torn pieces flapped gently against each other in the rain.

At least I knew where the sound was coming from.

I backed up against the tree trunk. "Norbert?" My stage whisper carried through the night, but no one answered. I tried again—louder—but there was still nothing. I jerked my phone downward, casting its glow on the ground. There they were, all over the mud at my feet: smudged Millennium Falcon imprints. I pointed my phone up. A small branch hung at an angle, newly broken. There were wet, muddy scrapes against the trunk.

Norbert had climbed this tree.

Norbert had gone into this building.

Shit.

I shoved my phone into my pocket—I was down to eleven percent battery life—and scrambled upward toward the closest branch. It wasn't the easiest thing in the world, climbing a tree in the dark, but the trunk was knotty with lots of solid bumps and thick twigs to grab. I was able to hoist myself onto the first branch and then another. If Norbert could do this, so could I. I wormed my way across the thick limb, extending over the deck. The branch bent a little as I reached the railing. When I made it onto the balcony, it sprang back into place with a rustling of leaves.

Up here, a full floor above the relative safety of the ground, the air smelled like fire and fear, and I knew not to call out for Norbert. I took a step toward the building. Something crunched beneath my foot. Light glinted from several places on the wooden balcony.

Shattered glass. Lots of it.

I stepped over the pile to the apartment's entrance. What had been a sliding door was now a jagged opening. It had been broken. Violently. The shards had exploded out in every direction. Faint starlight reflected on them.

Beyond the door was a pitch-black abyss. I pulled my phone back out, holding it before me as I stepped inside.

Ten percent battery life.

It had been a bedroom (this wasn't my awesome detective skills at work; there was a king-size bed pushed up against the wall). Now it was a deserted war zone.

From the middle of the room, I could see that there had once been something behind the sliding glass door:

a barricade to keep out intruders . . . or sunlight. It was made of thick iron, but it had been completely obliterated. Whatever had shattered the glass had blasted right through it too. Now that I was inside with my phone held high, I could see splinters of dark metal mixed with the glass shards.

This is so bad.

I cast my phone's light over the bed. It was simple: white wooden rail headboard, white sheets. It looked totally ordinary, like something you'd see in that discarded Target ad, except for one thing.

Splayed across it were ashes in the shape of a human body.

I leaned closer. It could have been my imagination, the darkness, whatever; there were what appeared to be charred pieces of bone mixed in with the ashes. A set of metal handcuffs was looped over the wooden slats at the head of the bed, the locks closed. On the white pillow right beneath them was a melted, misshapen circle of gold.

A ring. But destroyed, like the rest of the place.

I held my breath and reached out to touch it. It was smooth and cool, so I lifted it, hefting its weight. My mind flashed to Misty and that big golden ring on her finger . . .

Within the depths of the fourplex, there was a *clunk.* I shoved the ring into my pocket and looked around for something—anything—that could be used as a makeshift weapon. I found a jagged piece of iron on the floor and lifted it. It was about the size and shape of a long dagger, with some serious weight. I didn't know if I had it in me to use it against another human (or nonhuman), but it was better than nothing. I tiptoed toward the open door of the bedroom and peered out into the living area.

There *was* no living area.

My heart began to thud. The building wasn't even a fourplex. At least, not anymore. The inside of it had been ripped apart and crazily reassembled like a jigsaw puzzle from a lunatic's nightmare. I was looking at a corridor: sloping downward, lined by cavernous openings into other darkened rooms. Unlit lanterns swayed from the ceiling.

Below, I caught flickers of light. Candlelight. I felt like I'd stepped into a three-dimensional M. C. Escher painting, one that smelled like rotting garbage and was freaking terrifying.

And my cousin was somewhere inside.

I descended the corridor, holding my phone before me and testing each step before putting my weight onto it. The floor creaked, but it felt solid. I edged along until I reached the lip of the first opening: a gaping hole in the wall to my left. It was like a mouth. An uneven, black mouth waiting to swallow me whole.

I slid my foot ahead, hearing the scraping sound it made against the ground, and then shifted my weight forward.

One step.

I could do this. I could do this for Norbert.

I took another shuffling step, and then another. I was past the lip of the hole now. I had to look inside. I couldn't *not* look inside. So I slowly turned my head, my breath coming in shallow huffs, hearing it loud in my own ears along with the scraping of my foot moving forward . . .

Except I had stopped moving. I was frozen, staring into

utter blackness. And I was still hearing footsteps drag across the ground.

Somewhere nearby, someone else was walking.

It came down to this: I could keep sneaking along, trying not to be seen or heard even though I was pretty sure I had already been both seen *and* heard . . . or I could charge in like I owned the joint and deal with whatever came at me from the darkness. Both options sucked. I went with a third: the one that might get me out the quickest.

I raised my phone high in the air and yelled for my cousin: "Norbert!"

There was an awful pause in which the world stopped turning on its axis . . .

And then, the noises started.

From above me, there was a rustle. From the black hole to my left, a moan. From behind me, more scraping. But from down below, something much more welcome: an electronic squeal.

Norbert's key-chain alarm.

He was here. He was alive. Getting us out was all that mattered. I thrust my phone before me and headed downward as quickly as I dared. Passing one more awful, ripped-open hole of darkness, I briefly wondered if I had dipped below ground level. Was this the building's basement?

I turned a corner and found myself in a room made from stone. It could have been a wine cellar or a dungeon. It was empty except for two candles on a narrow wooden table and the most welcome sight I'd ever seen in my life: Norbert in a heap on the floor.

He blinked up at me. "Jillian, I found the lair."

I tried to swallow back the lump in my throat. He had no freaking clue how scared I'd been for him. "Good job," I managed, hoping Norbert wouldn't notice how my voice shook. "Are you okay?"

He set a hand on the side of his head and winced. "Not sure . . . I think something hit me."

I reached his side and helped him stagger to his feet. There was a dark smear along his temple and cheekbone. "Norbert, we really need to get out of here."

"First we should look around at—"

"No." My grip tightened around his shoulders. "I'm serious. We have to get out."

He forced a smile despite his pain. "Copy that," he said.

I grabbed his hand in my own, clutching my makeshift metal weapon in the other, and turned back toward the corridor ramping down from above. But something blocked our path. Norbert's fingers tightened around mine. I shoved myself in front of him. "Stay there," I murmured.

A flare of light erupted, so brilliant that I thrust the iron dagger in front of my face, temporarily blinded. Norbert and I reeled backward, blinking. A wave of something foul but oily—kerosene, I think—hit my nostrils and made me cough. I blinked furiously, my eyes watering against the light and the smell, until a man took shape.

He was seriously tall and muscular. He was also seriously naked. He held a torch, staring at us from the only exit.

"The Abomination is coming," he croaked.

We are starring in our very own horror movie.

"What is the Abomination?" Norbert whispered from behind me.

"Shh," I whispered back. I didn't want to question the large naked guy. I just wanted to get past him. His eyes were unfocused. He sniffed, like a bloodhound trying to find game. He cast his head about in jerky motions.

"The key," he said. "We want the key."

"I don't have it," I said, edging toward the exit.

"It is hidden."

"Um, who hid it?" Maybe if I pretended that we were having a normal conversation (like any part of this was normal), he'd drop his guard.

"The seven who didn't sleep," he said.

"Do you have any idea where they might have put it?" I asked. I vaguely remembered reading that if you are ever taken hostage, you should try to connect with your kidnappers so they'll think of you as a person and not kill you.

"The seven lied. The seven lied and one of them died. Six aren't enough to hide the key."

So much for connection. He was basically a naked, crazy Dr. Seuss. Awesome.

"What is the key for?" I asked, taking several more tiny steps in his direction, tugging Norbert along.

The man moved slightly to block the exit. "The key leads to the bridge."

My insides clenched.

His words were crazy, yes. But this time they were *familiar* crazy. For a dizzying instant, I was Norbert's age. Back in my mother's room. Back where she was chained to the bed so she wouldn't hurt herself again. Back where, no matter how hard I'd scrubbed, some of the walls were still streaked with bloodstains. I remembered her incoherence and the way she had shrieked until she'd lost her voice and could only ramble in whispers. The same words had tumbled out over and over and over before she died: "Burn the bridge, burn the bridge, burn the bridge . . ."

The man swung his large head toward me. "It is prophesied."

I hesitated. I wanted to know more. I *had* to know more—but first I had to get Norbert out of here. "Okay," I said to the man in what I hoped was a soothing voice. "I'll go look for the key."

He moved the torch in my direction, and this time we were close enough that I could see his face clearly. Patches of red whiskers dotted his skin. His bloodshot eyes bounced around the room, never seeming to fix on anything. "We will find the key! The key will lead us to the bridge! The armies will come—"

"I called the police," I shouted, just to shut him up. I raised my iron dagger again and tried to stop my voice from trembling. "They're on their way and we're just kids, so if you want a prayer of not getting locked up for the rest of your life, you'll back up and let us go."

The man surged forward, lowering his huge face right in front of mine. His breath was hot and smelled like cooking meat. "The world is splintering," he growled. "We won't stay out forever. Some of us are already here. Like me. Like her." He paused, sniffing at the air again. I tensed to make a run for it. "Her gold." He snarled, spittle flecking his curled lips. "You have her gold!"

Gold. The lump of gold in my pocket. Holy crap mother

of God, he could freaking smell the freaking gold in my freaking pocket . . .

No time to wonder how or why. My cousin and I were trapped in the presence of a muscled giant who—best-case scenario—was off-balance. A guy with a voice like a beast and a hair trigger.

I reached into my pocket for the circular gold lump. I held it level with the man's face. "You want this? Here you go, right here. Her gold."

The man's eyes tried to focus. I waved it around. He lurched forward, grabbing at it.

I whirled and threw the gold as hard as I could. It clinked against the far wall.

I spun back to the man. "Go get it," I told him. Clutching the iron dagger so hard that it cut into my skin, I darted to one side, pulling Norbert with me.

It was a super great escape plan, and it totally should have worked, except that the giant heaved first toward the gold, then back to block us. He came to a complete stop, staring at us with wide, angry, bloodshot eyes. He threw his head back and—there's really no other word for it—*howled* up into the darkness. The sound echoed back down to the floor where we stood. I felt Norbert crowd close behind me, his body sticky hot against mine.

"The Abomination!" The man's voice was so loud it hurt my eardrums. "Blood of the seventh! The Abomination is near!"

And then he went apeshit crazy, waving his torch around and shrieking.

I gave Norbert a hard yank toward the exit. The man

whipped around with a speed that shouldn't have been possible for his size. He hauled back and hurled his torch at us. I ducked, pulling Norbert down with me, and the torch flew over our heads. It hit something in the corner—a pile of debris—which burst into flames. Norbert and I screamed and careened away from it as the man charged toward us.

The whole world was fire and smoke and the thundering sound of the man's footsteps. I launched myself between him and Norbert, flung my hands up in the air, and just like outside Lilith's Bed, I *pushed*. Something erupted from me—an energy, a force, a wall of strength larger and stronger than the fire burning around us—and I felt it slam into him. He was hurled backward, crashing into the edge of the doorway. Norbert screamed again as the wooden doorframe cracked. The top half came loose, already smoking from the fire, and fell onto the man. It knocked him off his feet and pinned him to the floor, holding him there as the flames leapt to his body.

The man's screams mixed with Norbert's, and I tried to scream too, except I had gone weak, and my voice didn't work, and my legs wouldn't hold me up. I might have fallen, but my cousin caught me and dragged me toward the opening. As the flames jumped even higher, they illuminated something in the corner, beyond the debris. Something that had been previously hidden by the darkness.

No, not *something. Someone.*

Huddled in confusion and terror was the person whose face had haunted my every waking minute for the last few days:

Todd Harmon.

SIRENS HAD ALREADY BEGUN to pierce the air when Norbert and I emerged onto the smoldering balcony, a half-conscious Todd Harmon supported between us. We coughed, watery eyed, and staggered through the smoke pouring from the broken entrance at our backs. The heat grew in intensity, pushing us forward, trapping us against the railing. I looked down and relief washed through me.

Below were a pack of firefighters and cops. "They're up there!" one of them yelled.

I leaned over the edge, trying to scream that there was still someone inside. Instead I nearly puked up a lung.

"Go, go!" Norbert choked out.

I realized that he was trying to get me to jump over the side onto a trampoline below. No way. I'd go last. I dragged Todd Harmon toward the edge. Embers whizzed out of the building, landing like tiny red darts all around us as Norbert and I hefted Todd up and over the railing. *There he goes* . . .

The fall didn't look so bad. Not far at all. It looked almost *pleasant.* Todd landed smack in the middle of the trampoline. Firefighters cleared him off of it in a flash and stared back up at us, waving us to jump. "You go," I instructed Norbert between wheezes.

He looked like he was going to argue, but I gave him a hard shove and he obeyed. When he was safely on the ground, I followed. My insides heaved as I dropped, weightless, and I felt only a gentle smack on my back when

I landed. A firefighter gave me her hand to help me to the ground. And I was coughing again . . .

When I saw Sky.

He appeared out of nowhere at a dead run and launched himself straight at me, flinging his arms around my body and swinging me off my feet before I could stop him—or even remember that I wanted to stop him.

"Thank God, thank God, thank God," he kept saying into my hair.

Maybe I would have remembered his lies and pulled away from him. Or maybe I would have been too dizzy and exhausted to make a fuss. I'll never know because I didn't get a chance to make a decision. Before I could say a word or take a stand, the building exploded.

TWENTY-FOUR

Ambulance rides are never fun, but a hospital is all things I hate: sterile to the point of anal, everything placed at right angles to everything else, riddled with unhelpful employees using inscrutable medical terminology. Worse yet, this particular hospital was full of sanctimonious cops.

I experienced the great joy of being lectured by one of them about the dangers of exploring abandoned buildings.

His name was Officer Simon (his cop badge was very shiny, so his name was hard to miss). He was young, maybe five years older than me, with round red cheeks and blue eyes that blinked a lot.

"Maybe you think this is a game . . ." Officer Simon was saying.

I pretended to listen as we stood near the third-floor nurses' station, waiting for updates on the conditions of Todd Harmon (smoke inhalation), Norbert Cade (mild concussion), and Sky Ramsey (general assholery—at least as far as I was concerned). It was the first time I'd been allowed out of bed.

"But you should consider any property with which you are not personally familiar to be inherently dangerous."

"I'm sorry." I hoped my apology would put an end to the harangue so I could go check up on Sky. And then perhaps murder him. A few minutes earlier, I'd caught a glimpse of him—up and about and out of his hospital room—but somehow he had managed to duck away, leaving me to take the brunt of Officer Simon's speechifying.

"Methamphetamine labs contain poisonous and flammable materials," Officer Simon informed me. "That is why criminals often do their cooking in abandoned houses. You kids are lucky you got out of there before it blew up. You could have been killed. At the very least, you were illegally trespassing."

Leave it to Misty to pick a meth lab as a place to live. Or maybe that was *why* she had picked it. So she could blow the place up and make a quick getaway. The irony was almost tragic: she herself had been reduced to ashes before she could torch her "lair."

Still, I bristled. "We were trying to help someone."

Officer Simon glanced across the waiting area. I followed his pitying eyes to an open recovery room, where Todd Harmon lay in bed, gazing up at Corabelle. She was perched beside him, her back to us, holding his hand. As we watched, she leaned over and nuzzled against his neck.

I had caught sight of her face when she'd sprinted through on her arrival not long ago. She had looked awful. Nothing but stringy hair and smeared makeup and sagging clothes. She still may have been a rank bitch to me, but there was one thing I *could* say about Corabelle

LaCaze: she wasn't a liar. She really *had* wanted her boy-friend back.

Maybe it was the Todd-Corabelle snuggle fest, but Officer Simon softened. "Well, you did one thing right today, miss."

He gave me a nod and walked away, adjusting his belt as he went. He'd barely disappeared around the corner when Sky appeared behind me. He grabbed my upper arm, pulling me to face him. "I have to tell you some-thing," he said. His voice was low and urgent.

I yanked myself backward, out of his grasp. "Don't touch me."

Yes, I needed to tell him what a horrible person he was, that he had turned my feelings into a joke, and that he'd made me a pawn in his sick game. But I needed to wait. If I said those words out loud right then, I might start crying. So instead, I whirled away and marched across the waiting area toward Norbert's room. Allowed or not, I was going to visit him.

When I came in, he was sitting up in bed. His head was wrapped with a thick bandage. There was a bloodstain on it. "I'm fine," he told me, reading a look I wished I'd hidden. "Head wounds bleed a lot. It's nothing. Don't freak out."

I forced a smile. "The doctors say you have a mild con-cussion," I told him. "You'll get discharged any time now."

Sky burst in behind me. "You guys have to listen," he said. "Where's—"

"Shut up!" I turned around with a snarl. "This is family only. Stay away from me and my cousin."

Sky gaped at me. "What's going on? I'm trying to help you! Everything I do is to help you!"

"Oh, really?" I shouted back. "You know what was super *helpful*? When you snuck my obituary into my locker! That was wildly helpful! I'm so grateful for your wonderful, generous *help*!" I stopped, breathing hard, knowing my face was flushed, hoping against hope that the floodgates behind my eyes wouldn't burst in front of Sky-the-Liar.

"That was *you*?" said Norbert weakly.

Sky blinked at him, then at me. He had no response.

"Why were you trying to scare me?" I asked. "I didn't even *know* you! Did someone at school put you up to it?"

"No!"

"Oh, so it was just fun to terrorize the daughter of your hero?"

"Jillian, stop." Sky grabbed me by the arms. I tried to shake away from him but he hung on. "I will explain everything, I promise, but right now we have a bigger problem than your obituary." He let go of me and held up a cell phone.

Correction: *my* cell phone. The shattered screen was a dead giveaway.

"Give it back!" I grabbed at it, but Sky held it out of my reach. "How did you get that?"

"I took it from your pocket outside Misty's lair."

"Ballsy," said Norbert.

Of course. I remembered how Sky had thrown his arms around me right before the building exploded. It hadn't been to save me; it had been to rob me. I felt like there was a thick rubber band squeezing the blood out of my heart. "So you're a liar *and* a thief."

"No! I'm a . . ." Sky struggled for the right word. "Detective. Researcher. Historian."

"Dick."

"Call me whatever you want, but I needed to talk to your father."

It always comes back to my father.

I shrunk away from him, backing toward Norbert's bed. "I *had* to steal your phone," Sky went on. "I knew you wouldn't give it to me. The only reason I didn't tell you until now is because it was out of juice, so I had to go plug it in. Your dad is going to send a file. It should be here any second."

I glanced at Norbert. "I can't do this anymore," I told him. "I'll call you later. I'm getting a cab."

"Hold on." Norbert leaned forward and caught my wrist. "What did Uncle Lewis say? Jillian, wait."

I waited, but only because my cousin had a mild concussion and I thought maybe I should be sweet to him. He let go.

Sky waved my stolen phone at me. "Dr. Cade said to tell you in no uncertain terms that you are *not* to go succubus hunting. They are extremely dangerous because of their addiction."

Norbert frowned. "*Their* addiction? I thought men got addicted to *them*?"

"It goes both ways." Sky's words came quickly. "Jillian, that's what Dr. Cade said. Succubi can go through life just being generally beautiful and feeding off the desire of random men who pass by, but what really satisfies a succubus is establishing a mutual addiction. It's like the relationship between bees and flowers. Bees get nectar from flowers, and at the same time, help them pollinate."

I shook my head. I couldn't listen to this. Not now.

"So which one is helping the other pollinate?" my cousin asked.

"Both. Succubi have black, forked tongues." Sky paused for a split second to shoot me a knowing look. "They're tipped with tiny fangs. When a succubus kisses a man, she can inject her poison—her drug—into his mouth. After that, he's gone. He thinks he loves her so much that he'll die if they're not together."

I shook my head again, edging toward the door. "That doesn't make any sense. What is the succubus addicted to?"

"Desire," said Sky.

I looked over at Norbert. He nodded slowly, brow furrowed under his bandage, as if putting the pieces together. "So that's what happened to Misty. She was addicted to Todd's desire."

"Right," Sky told him. "Once a succubus injects a man, his addiction manifests as desire, and the succubus *needs* that particular man's desire. They're imprinted on each other. If she can't get it, she loses her beauty and her power. Eventually, she goes crazy and dies."

I wanted to leave. No, I wanted to slap him, then leave. But my mind was spinning, flashing back to Lilith's Bed, to the rage in Misty's face when she barked that Todd Harmon belonged to *her*. "So Misty picked Todd and stuck her forked tongue in his mouth," I said. "He got addicted to her, and she got addicted to him. That's why he ditched his girlfriend and his roommates and his job? So he could fake (above CADE)

follow a succubus to South LA where they could both be all addicty with each other?"

My phone vibrated. I took the opportunity to snatch it out of Sky's hand. "Allow me," I told him, swiping at the cracked screen. First thing I needed to do after kicking Sky's ass and getting paid: buy a new phone.

There it was: an email from my father.

"What is it?" asked Norbert.

"The subject says *research notes*," I told him.

"Read it out loud," Sky said. He blocked my exit. "Please."

I didn't want him listening to my father's words, but I also thought reading the email out loud would speed things up, so I touched the message. It was long. I took a deep breath and read: *"Succubi are highly territorial loners. Each one behaves as a queen bee who will tolerate no rivals. In cities, the size of a domain can be up to a dozen miles in diameter, as the succubi are few and far between. Her drones are all human: female supplicants and the men upon whom she feeds. The only reason she will venture beyond her own boundaries is to take a rival down. Stealing the imprinted man of another succubus will cripple the succubus from whom he is stolen. This is why a succubus will often imprint a man and feed off him for a while, but then kill him herself before he can be stolen by another."*

The message ended there. Of course there wasn't even a *Love, Dad*. This was a research file.

I was silent. So were Sky and Norbert. Maybe they were thinking the same thing I was: there *was* something here, a connection to all of this madness. But the puzzle didn't seem to be complete.

Sky's eyes locked on mine. "It's got to be ten miles from Misty's lair in Leimert Park to where she hung out in Little Tokyo."

"Neither is anywhere near the Valley," I said.

And that's when the pieces finally clicked together. That's when it took shape: the whole picture. That's when the horror started rising inside me.

"It's out of her domain," said Sky.

"There's only one reason she would have been in the Valley," Norbert added. His voice had gone thin and tight. "To take down a rival. To steal a man."

Sky nodded. "Not just any man. An imprinted man."

I wanted to contribute to the conversation, but words wouldn't come out. My gaze flew back to Norbert as he spoke:

"Misty grabbed Todd Harmon from another succubus."

I sucked in a breath. The burst of oxygen kicked my brain into gear. When I spoke, my voice sounded hollow in my ears. "A succubus named Corabelle LaCaze."

That's when we heard the beeping.

TWENTY-FIVE

Sky and I raced out of Norbert's room—straight into a stampede of doctors and nurses. All were racing toward the beeping—toward Todd Harmon's room—yelling things like "Code blue!" and "Crash cart!" The beeping was shrill, and it was loud, and it wouldn't stop.

Then Corabelle appeared. She floated right out of Todd's door, through the onslaught, and into the waiting area. Her hair was in the same ponytail that I'd seen when she raced in, but it didn't look the same. No longer greasy, no longer lank, it was once again the bouncy beautiful blond wave that it had always been. Her skin had cleared up too, and her eyes—as they found mine—were a gorgeous, crystal blue.

Corabelle was back.

We froze, staring at her. Her smile wasn't scary or bitchy at all. It was dazzling and enticing. The kind of friendly smile you wanted to return, that you almost couldn't *help* but return.

"Thank you," Corabelle said to me. "Thank you for finding him."

I nodded. She was beautiful and vital again, but she didn't look like a succubus. Or at least not like what I now believed succubi to look like. Corabelle wasn't as tall as Misty; her skin wasn't as pale or freakishly luminous. Most telling of all, Sky didn't seem to be losing his mind from her presence. I marched straight toward her, ignoring the chaos around us. Sky tried to stop me, but I twisted away.

"Stick out your tongue," I ordered her.

Without missing a beat, she did it, as if I'd made the most normal request in the world in response to the gratitude she'd shown for my finding her boyfriend. She opened her perfect, pink lips and stuck out her perfect, pink tongue.

Okay, that would have been too easy.

"What happened to Todd?" I demanded. "Is he going to be okay?"

Before Corabelle could answer, Sky spun me around to face him. "Stop this. Maybe your dad was wrong about the tongue thing."

"Since when do you doubt the great Dr. Cade?"

I turned back to Corabelle, but she wasn't there anymore. There was a flash of blond at the corner, and then she was gone.

I would have chased after her, but unfortunately my arms were pinned at my sides by one of Aunt Aggie's hugs.

"Angel love!" she shrieked into my ear.

Sky was trapped too. Uncle Edmund had grabbed him by the shoulders. "Where's Norbert?" he boomed.

I wrestled away from my aunt while Sky shook free and

pointed in the direction of Norbert's room. "Over there," he said. "And sorry but—"

"We have to go!" I finished for him.

Sky bolted from the waiting area. I should have been right behind him, but Uncle Edmund pounced on me.

"Hold it."

"Please," I gasped, struggling against his grasp. "You don't understand. I'll be fine. I have to do this one thing. It's really important. I'll come right back."

My uncle was strong. Stronger than I'd realized. I couldn't even wriggle.

"No," he snapped. "Jillian, this is very serious. We promised your father that we would keep you safe. And we always assumed you would do the same. We trusted you, Jilly. We trusted you with our son."

Aunt Aggie stood by his side. Her relief had fallen away. Now her face was creased with anger. "Is it true you've been taking Norbert to explore crack houses in Leimert Park?"

I almost said, *It wasn't a crack house; it was a meth lab.* I bit my lip. Probably not a distinction they'd care to make. Besides, neither was true. Of course they were pissed. I had put Norbert in danger. I felt terrible too, but I didn't have time to apologize or make amends. Corabelle had escaped and I needed to find her. Succubus or not, she *was* dangerous.

"Clear!" came a shout from Todd Harmon's room. There was a jolt, followed by a high-pitched whine. No more beeping. Just an even tone.

I felt that rubber band pull around my heart again.

I was responsible for this. If I hadn't found him in that basement, he wouldn't be here right now, and Corabelle wouldn't have hurt him. I had to convince my aunt and uncle to let me go.

Maybe I could. Maybe I had a trump card to play.

I looked at my uncle. "Listen, I get why you're mad. I get it because I trusted *you*. And I know you know that I would never hurt Norbert. So now that we're on the subject of trust, let me ask you something. Do I have a sister?"

Uncle Edmund went ashen. In seconds. Whiter than Misty. His grip loosened. A puff of air escaped Aunt Aggie's mouth.

So. The trump card worked. It was all I needed to know.

"Go see Norbert," I said, and then I raced away.

THE DOORS OF TWO elevators at the end of the hallway were closed. The lights above them showed that one was on the top floor, the floor above us. The other was headed down. That had to be Sky. I would have done the same, guessing Corabelle had taken the stairs to throw us off, and was trying to flee the way she'd come in: out the front door.

I jabbed the up arrow. From the roof, I could both avoid Sky *and* get a bird's-eye view of the surrounding streets. Maybe I could even spot her. *Screw it.* I bolted for the stairs and took them two at a time, racing up to the roof door. It was marked EMERGENCY EXIT ONLY. I held my breath as I pressed the thick metal bar . . . and no alarms blared.

Amazing. Something had actually gone my way.

I stepped out onto the roof, let go of the door, and then reached back to snag it before it could close. It's not like

I'd never seen a movie before. The last thing I wanted was to get trapped. I wasn't carrying anything besides my nearly destroyed phone, so I took off one boot and used it to wedge the door open. I would have wadded up my T-shirt and used that, but then I'd be a girl on a hospital roof in a bra. The clock on that scenario would be a short one, and I'd end up talking to Officer Simon again.

It wasn't until I was outside that I remembered that it was the middle of the night. Floodlights illuminated a giant white cross with an *H* at its center. A helicopter landing pad, maybe? It was the only part of the roof that was lit up. Nothing but murky shadows everywhere else. From where I was standing, I could see a rusty red rail along the edge of the roof. I set my hand on it and followed it into the gloom, letting my fingers trail over the scabby roughness. To my left something was making a loud whirring sound: giant fans and air-conditioning vents.

I reached a corner and peered out over the edge. I wasn't sure of the hospital's exact location, but in the direction I was looking—which I thought was north—I could see the Santa Monica Freeway. I had to be in Baldwin Hills or nearby. When I looked straight down (which made me dizzy), I could see the entrance to an underground parking garage and a busy street. Lots of pedestrians, even at this hour. Lights at every intersection.

I didn't see a gleaming blond ponytail. I didn't see anyone running away. I didn't—

"Looking for this?"

I flinched. Corabelle stood right beside me, holding up my boot. I made a reflexive grab for it, but Corabelle chucked it over the railing. It fell to an unoccupied patch of pavement.

"Hey, that's a real Doc Marten!"

She laughed. Her laughter was easy, relaxed, almost musical. "And I'm a real succubus," she said. "Boo!"

I tried to back up, but I was already pressed against the railing. "Are you trying to scare me?" I asked. A lame question, yes, but also an effort to buy time while I struggled through the information I'd received that day: Sky's role in my obituary, Uncle Edmund's knowledge of my sister, now Corabelle claiming to be a succubus.

"Honestly, you scare *me*," she said with a disappointed sigh. "You're rude, and gross, and you never say anything interesting. It's like you've never even *seen* good makeup or a push-up bra. Being stuck babysitting you has been the assignment from hell."

I stole a peek at the street below. My lone boot sat there in a pale circle of lamplight. "Does 'from hell' mean that you're giving me a compliment? Seeing as you're . . . you know."

"Ugh, you're not even funny," she said. "You should drop the attempts at humor. And seriously, a little mascara would really open up your eyes."

"Look, I'd love to trade beauty tips with you, but I think we can come up with a better topic of conversation." Inside my head, a bulb brightened. "Like how you *can't* be a succubus because I've seen you in sunlight."

Corabelle threw back her head and laughed again. Clear and loud and pretty, like a church bell. "Yeah, well, I've seen you in geometry class. Doesn't mean you like it."

"So you're saying succubi don't burn in the sun?"

"Shit, Jillian." Corabelle rolled her huge blue eyes. "You of all people should know how rumors work. Once one gets started, people will believe all kinds of crazy things. Now imagine a rumor mill that's been around for an eternity."

I jabbed a finger at her. "Fine, but I've seen your tongue. It's totally pink and totally normal and totally human. So that proves it."

"You're clueless."

"You're a poser."

Corabelle's smile shifted. Her gaze hardened even as her mouth very slowly turned up at the corners.

She took a step toward me. I swear the shadows around us deepened. Corabelle couldn't have possibly grown because my eyes stayed at the same level with hers as they had been, but it *felt* like she got bigger. It seemed like I was looking up at her now. But maybe I was cowering. She leaned close to me and spoke in a gentle whisper. "I know that you are tremendously stupid. But surely you have enough brains to realize that *you*, like most of humanity, don't believe in us because *that's the way we want it*. The more legends that swirl around us, the less real we become."

Cold sweat broke out along my hairline. My mind flashed back to Sky's words about Santa Claus. Someone, somewhere, in the past had been real. But the eternal rumor mill had turned that real, charitable person into a jolly myth.

"You've said it yourself: we don't exist." Corabelle's voice was too deep, her eyes too intense, her stare too menacing for her to be the girl I thought I'd known.

I put up my hands in what I thought was a pacifying gesture. "Hey, I'm not saying you don't exist—"

"Shh," she whispered. Her fingers encircled my wrists.
Her grip was strong. Stronger than Uncle Edmund's. Inhu-
manly strong. Corabelle was still smiling as she moved her
face even closer to mine. "Here's the thing. You're making
an assumption about me. About us. About how we are."

She parted her glossy, plump lips and stuck her tongue
out at me again. For a second, all was okay in the world. The
hot, popular girl from high school was just an immature
bitch, trying to freak me out. She was not a man-sucking
demon. Life still made a tiny bit of sense.

But then, from underneath that tongue—one that
would have sent any straight high-school boy into a hor-
monal frenzy—another shape darted out.

It was long and thin and black.

And it ended in a fork.

Corabelle had a second tongue.

TWENTY-SIX

I'm not sure how much time passed after the worst version of show-and-tell I'd ever experienced. I do know that I briefly considered throwing myself after my boot.

"You really don't know, do you?" Corabelle asked.

I shook my head. She was right, whatever she meant. I knew now that I knew almost nothing. I had stumbled into one of those nightmares where you're being chased but you can't run fast enough because the whole world has turned to mud. Except this wasn't a nightmare. I was awake, on the edge of a roof, face-to-face with . . . Corabelle. Maybe that's why I said what I said. What came out of my mouth in a burst of whispered honesty was this: "I thought none of it was real."

"You're the worst." Corabelle mimicked my head shake. "I have to spend two years of my life watching you when you've never even *heard* of the Abomination, and now you're trying to engage my services as a tutor? Please. I'm a valuable commodity. I didn't awaken for this."

"Watching me? Awaken from what?" The questions fell

from my mouth in the order they sprung from my stupefied brain.

"From sleep, stupid." She looked me up and down. "I should throw you off this roof right now. I'm not falling apart anymore. I'm back on my game. You can be dead along with Todd."

I pushed aside my guilt and sadness and remorse over Todd (who would now be forever falsely known as a dead meth addict, not as the naïve pre-med student who got caught up in something he'd never imagined). I scrambled for ideas that might possibly save me. "But what if someone steals your *next* guy? That happens all the time to succubi, right? I can help get *that* guy back. I can be like your safety net."

Too bad Dad wasn't there. Or Norbert. Or even Sky. I was having a conversation, in English, on a rooftop, with someone who killed people and had a venomous second tongue. This was now my life.

"Imprinted energy is more satisfying," Corabelle informed me with a shrug. "Imagine eating salad all the time. Sure, there are decent salads, and you'd be fine and alive, but at some point, you'd be sick to death of leafy greens. All you'd want would be a piece of freaking chocolate."

"So Todd was your chocolate?"

She turned away and slumped against the railing, resting her forearms on its top and gazing out over the city lights. "Yeah, he was my chocolate. I'll kinda miss him."

I stared at her. "But we found him alive. You could have *kept* him."

Corabelle sighed. "He was a liability. He made me weak. Which was not good, since I was awakened to watch *you*."

"In school?" I whispered, baffled.

"Yeah, and it was crap. No other succubus got stuck in stupid high school for two years. I ended up being a part of it. I hated you all, but I got used to being one of you. I started to *feel* like one of you."

Sadly, I knew what Corabelle meant. It wasn't much different than what Sky had been saying about Santa Claus. I had spent so much time cultivating "Jillian Cade," unfeeling badass, that the image had started to become real. I believed in my own myth too.

"Ugh, it's such a weakness," said Corabelle. "All that love crap and the thing where you want to be nice to someone else and pretend to listen to them about their boring day."

An image flashed into my mind. It was the photo that I'd seen in Todd's room, the one of Corabelle hiking. The one where she had looked happy . . .

Then Corabelle's fingers tightened around the railing, and she snapped off the top bar like it was a popsicle stick. I jerked backward as she whirled to me, holding what was now essentially a rusted metal club. "My gifts were being squandered," she informed me. "Sure, I went against regulations, and sure, I engaged the Abomination—"

That word again. It made it through to my brain despite the loud beating in my ears.

"—but it's not like I had a choice! It's not like I volunteered to be on guard duty. *He* made me!" Corabelle was becoming more agitated. Frenzied, really. She bore down on me. "This is all *your* fault. You don't deserve to be here! You were never *supposed* to be here!"

I tripped on something behind me and fell backward, landing on the pavement by the edge of the roof. Loose pieces of concrete dug into my palms. I tried to scuttle away from her like a crab. Corabelle raised the metal bar over my head, and the sound of my pulse turned into a rushing stream, a river, a waterfall. It was deafening, thunderous, way too loud to make any sense, and Corabelle *had* to hear it because it was booming out of me, over us both.

Corabelle froze, except for her golden-fire hair whipping in the wind. The wind that had suddenly erupted around us. We looked skyward at the same moment—the moment we were bathed in a blinding glare of light.

It wasn't my pulse, after all. It was a helicopter. A sleek, black helicopter. It settled atop the *H* painted in the roof's center. Blades still whirring, its door opened and stairs descended.

A dark angel stepped out.

At least that's what I thought in that moment.

Corabelle LaCaze was a succubus. So calling this guy a "dark angel" (in my brain) made sense, given the circumstances, which didn't. Besides, he wasn't a doctor; this wasn't a medevac chopper. He was a tall, slender guy in black, loose-fitting clothing. He could have been in high school, or he could have been ten years older; it was impossible to tell. His face was unlined, blemish-free, framed with dark, straight, chin-length hair. His cheekbones alone screamed "angel." Or the world's most terrifying *GQ* model. He started toward us.

fake

"Hide me," Corabelle yelped.

Now I had to process that *she* was scared. Corabelle: a fiend, who just a second ago was about to kill me. I stared at the guy as he drew close enough for me to see his gray, almond-shaped eyes. I scrambled to my feet, making an attempt to smooth my hair. After all, I had a pretty good guess at who was now looming over us, all dark and chiseled and intimidating. I stuck one hand out toward him.

"I'm Jillian Cade," I said. "But you probably already knew that."

He didn't take my hand, so I dropped it. He shot a glance at Corabelle before turning back to me. In a smooth, melodious voice, he asked, "And who do you think I am?"

"The Abomination?" It came out like a question.

Corabelle flinched. "I did not tell her that," she said. "I swear I never said that—"

"No," he interrupted in that soft voice. "I am not the Abomination."

I couldn't stop myself from saying it: "You're not?"

"No," he said again. He took a step closer and peered down into my eyes. "Jillian Cade, *you* are the Abomination."

CORABELLE TOOK THIS OPPORTUNITY to bargain with whoever this guy was. He was not the Abomination, because that delightful moniker apparently belonged to me. Now that I heard it, it *was* a perfect summation of the image I'd created at school. The fake/real me.

"I know I broke the rules, but I had a really good reason," Corabelle was saying. "You have to hear me out—"

"The job you were given was a simple one," he interrupted. "Keep quiet. Watch the Abomination. Report any signs of self-awareness."

I was self-aware enough to know I needed to get out of there. If Corabelle LaCaze was afraid of Mr. Tall-Dark-and-Terrifying, then it only made sense for me to be too. My gaze slid over to the emergency door where I had emerged onto the roof. Surely someone else would come up here. A freaking *helicopter* had landed. All I had to do was live long enough for backup to arrive, right?

"I was smart to engage the Abomination," Corabelle argued. "We don't know what using her powers could lead to."

He turned to me. "Have you heard the call of our kind? Are you pulled in the direction of the bridge?"

The bridge.

I squeezed my eyes shut, trying to block out memories of my mother writhing on the floor, a corkscrew of screaming insanity.

"Jillian Cade," Dark Angel said.

My eyes popped open.

"You have never been educated about your heritage—"

"Allow me," Corabelle interrupted. "Jillian Cade, you're the daughter of a traitor and should have been killed at birth."

I let the words sink in. I wasn't sure what she meant by "traitor" (Dad was a run-of-the-mill con man), but the second part felt overly harsh, even for someone who wanted me dead. *I* couldn't help who'd given birth to me. I hadn't *asked* for my family, not by a long shot.

"Quiet," Dark Angel said. "Killing the Abomination could destroy the bridge."

"We don't *need* armies to cross over," Corabelle retorted. "Enough of us have awakened to *be* the army. Let's take control for once and—"

"You don't make decisions," he told her. "You receive instructions."

Corabelle trembled. "You are wasting my innumerable talents," she said through gritted teeth before whirling in my direction. "I told you. This is *your* fault." Her fingers whitened around the rusted metal railing she was still holding.

I glanced between the two of them. "I don't even know what's going on," I whispered. "How can anything be my fault?"

"Your mother betrayed the Pact," said Corabelle. The way she pronounced it, the word definitely had a capital P. "She was one of the seven traitors."

Wait. *Mom* was the traitor Corabelle was talking about?

Corabelle glared at me. "She stayed awake and hidden when all else slept. She was the breaker of laws and the destroyer of worlds. She coupled with a *human*."

"Enough!" thundered Dark Angel.

But Corabelle's anger issues were stronger than her ability to censor herself. "*You* were the disgusting result," she finished.

Not that her words were necessary. No, it was all clear: I'd had the pieces wrong before. I had missed this entire puzzle. So had Norbert. So had . . .

Actually, I had no idea what Sky had missed or what he knew. But at least now *I* knew a few things.

My mother: not a human.

My father: the human she had coupled with.

Me: the result.

The Abomination.

Corabelle lunged forward and jabbed my cheekbone with the metal. The jab was hard enough to snap my head back, hard enough to snap my brain back to my present danger. "We're all supposed to be thankful for the awakenings, but . . ."

The guy—Dark Angel or whatever he was—stepped in. He plucked the railing out of Corabelle's hands as easily as if it were a rattle and she were a crabby toddler. She gasped and leapt backward, but he was faster. In a single step, he'd seized her. Behind us, the helicopter's blades gained speed. Dark Angel lifted Corabelle in his arms and carried her to the railing.

She twisted her neck to look back at me. "He's going to kill me," she said. "He wants you to watch."

I wasn't sure what to say. She was right: it definitely seemed that way.

"Are you?" I asked Dark Angel, mopping at the blood I felt trickling from my cheekbone.

He nodded.

Against all odds, I felt a surge of indignation. Even . . . yes, *sympathy.* I knew what Corabelle was feeling, because she'd made me feel the same way. No one deserves to be murdered in cold blood. Not even a horrible, life-sucking succubus.

"Maybe you don't have to do that," I said. "We can all work this out, right, Corabelle?"

Corabelle shook her head. "God, you're such a human." It was definitely not a compliment.

"I'm trying to help you here."

"Well, don't," she snapped. "I didn't get awakened just so my last moments could be spent accepting help from the half-human Abomination."

Dark Angel looked at me. I kept my eyes on Corabelle.

"You loved Todd," I said, taking a step toward her and ignoring him. "I saw a picture he took of you. It was the only time I've ever seen you look happy."

"Yeah, well, you people are contagious. Hanging out with you all the time, your humanity rubs off. That was the part of me that loved him. The part that was human. The part that was weak."

"We can't help being weak," I said, coming closer. "We can't help that we're not as strong as you."

"It's not your bodies that are weak." Corabelle's nostrils flared. She zeroed in on the wound on my cheek. The one she had given me. "Blood of the seventh," she hissed. She bared her teeth, and her black tongue darted out between them. "I will kill you."

"Please don't," I whispered.

"She won't," Dark Angel said. And with that, he threw Corabelle off the roof.

FOR AS LONG AS I live—whether it's the threatened six months or another eighty years—I will never forget the sound of Corabelle's final scream. It was high and loud and terrified.

It sounded human.

It ended in a crushing thump when she hit the concrete far below.

Dark Angel gazed down at me. "It was justice," he said by way of explanation.

I looked up at Corabelle's murderer, this too-good-looking guy holding the keys to my muddled history. My teeth chattered against each other, despite the warm still-summer air. "What now?"

He shrugged. "Now someone else will have to watch you."

I opened my mouth to ask a question—to ask *every* question—but he was already heading back to the helicopter. A moment later, it lifted into the sky. The lights and the deafening whir faded. I was alone on the roof.

Me. The Abomination.

TWENTY-SEVEN

Aggie and Edmund had an older-model Honda Civic with four doors and five seats. The car's interior carried the fragrance of apples and peanut butter. I wondered if they had bought it used from another family or if Norbert was just one of those guys who always smells like a little kid.

Uncle Edmund was silent at the wheel, as was Aunt Aggie in the passenger seat. I was silent in the back beside Norbert—who was still sporting the white bandage over one side of his head—as we drove up the 405 to the Valley.

I probably needed a bandage too. For more than my injuries. But when I had descended from the roof, I'd refused all medical assistance. I sent Sky a text with my last scrap of battery power. Then I went straight to Aggie and Edmund and Norbert. As far as the hospital staff was concerned, I was fine and I wanted to go home.

At least half of that was true.

Norbert had long since fallen asleep. He flopped against me when we made the turn onto Exposition. I didn't mind the sweaty weight of his head on my shoulder. I didn't even mind that we'd left my GTO in Leimert Park.

As we crested the top of the hill and saw the lights of the San Fernando Valley sparkling before us, I could hear Aunt Aggie talking softly to Uncle Edmund. "You know she's going to tell Norbert. That boy dies of withdrawal, and then his girlfriend commits suicide off the hospital roof. It's all too terrible for words. We have to . . ."

Uncle Edmund murmured something I couldn't hear. My aunt settled back into her seat. The exits slid past us in silence.

I wondered if he'd said something about my sister.

But I was too exhausted and numb and bruised to ask about her or my obituary or to find out if anyone in the car had heard of the Abomination (otherwise known as me). Besides, even though my cousin was drooling—just a little—on my shirt, I didn't want to wake him up.

Maybe I fell asleep too, because suddenly we were parked in Norbert's driveway. I allowed myself to be taken inside, to be led down the stairs and tucked into a sleeping bag laid across the couch in their basement. I breathed in the comforting mustiness, closed my eyes, and drifted away.

THE NEXT MORNING, AUNT Aggie called the school office and said that Norbert and I were sick. She told us that education was important and she didn't believe in fibs, but this one time only, she would tell a lie.

"It's okay to take a day off when you need it. Sometimes lies are necessary."

She didn't notice my sudden smile at this explanation. Or maybe she did. She didn't smile back.

After an utterly silent breakfast of scrambled eggs and cinnamon rolls, Uncle Edmund said he'd drive me back to Leimert Park to get my car. I saw Aunt Aggie's lips purse, and I gathered that she'd already registered a protest about it. "I don't see why you can't—"

Uncle Edmund cut her off. "Jilly will feel better when her wheels are at home."

"Then why don't we all go get her car?"

"I want some time alone with my niece," Uncle Edmund said. That put an end to that.

AMONG ALL THE FAKE people in my life, of all the people living lies, I still respected Uncle Edmund more than most. He'd lied to protect me—and that helped, or it would once I knew the reasons—but mostly he'd lied to protect Norbert. That I could understand. Sometimes a lie is indeed necessary. Now I just needed to know why. That *he* could understand.

We were inching south on the 405 when he finally spoke. "Your aunt doesn't want me to talk to you about your sister."

"Why?"

"Because it's very sad," he said, careful to stare straight ahead at the sluggish crawl of cars. "She's afraid of what it will make you think of your parents."

My mouth went dry. I didn't answer.

"My brother was a mess," Uncle Edmund explained. I could tell from the fidgety way he spoke, fingers tapping the steering wheel, that he was embarking on a speech he'd rehearsed many times in his head but had never wanted to give in real life. "He ran away from home all the time when he was your age. Got in trouble with the police. Drugs. And girls. There were always girls around . . ."

I didn't want to know about my father's sordid escapades. The only thing I cared about was my sister, but Uncle Edmund needed to get there in his own time.

"Go on," I told him.

"Everything changed when he met your mom. As far as I'm concerned, he would be dead if it wasn't for Gwen. He grew up because he made a *choice* to grow up. He grew up for her."

I blinked back the sudden heat behind my eyes. If he grew up for her, why couldn't he be there for me?

"But he also left us for her," my uncle said, as if reading my mind. "We wouldn't see him for months at a time, sometimes years, and then we started hearing about this stuff he was teaching, this crazy business he was in. Our parents didn't like it, but me and Aggie . . . we didn't care." He cast a sideways glance at me. "She believes in it, you know."

I nodded. It made sense. It actually went a long way toward explaining why Norbert was the way he was—a fellow believer living a nice, sheltered life. "Do *you*?"

"I think sometimes it's better not to know."

Right. I couldn't help but think that this too was something he'd prepared for a worst-case scenario. Something to soothe Norbert or me, without sugarcoating the truth. Why not? Everything would be a lot easier right now if I wasn't aware of any of it either. If I could just tootle on

fake

with my life. If I could go back to being a fake detective solving fake cases.

"Your parents didn't tell us they were expecting you," Uncle Edmund said. "They had already moved to California, and we only found out after you'd been born. They sent a picture. You were cute, by the way. Bald, but cute."

"Thanks."

His grip tightened on the wheel. "Rosemary . . ."

My sister.

"She was born a year later. Again, they hadn't told us she was coming, so we had no idea it would be a bad time to take a cross-country road trip and surprise them. We surprised them, all right. Rosemary was two weeks old and . . . there was something wrong with her."

"What do you mean?"

"At first Lew and Gwen didn't want to show her to us, but there we were in the living room, and you were so little and toddling around, bumping into things. They couldn't exactly say no." Uncle Edmund coughed into his hand. "They swore us to secrecy. They said we couldn't tell anyone there was a new baby, and then they brought her downstairs." He stopped talking while he concentrated on merging onto the 10 going east. Once we were securely in a lane, he continued. "Her skin was so pale. Too pale, almost like glass. You could see her veins through it, and her hair and her eyes were white."

I swallowed, trying to shut out the memory of Misty's skin. "Her eyes?"

"All of them, pupils and everything. She'd turn her head to follow noise, but then it seemed like . . ." Again, he paused. "It seemed like she was looking *through* you. I can't explain it."

"What happened to her?" It was hard to get the words out past the lump in my throat. Not only was the obituary right about one thing—that there had really been a sister—but I had actually *known* her. Maybe my parents had sat beside me on the couch and helped me hold her, this strange and scary and tiny baby. Maybe they had let me give her a bottle. Maybe we'd all sung a song to her. I wished I could remember.

"They sent her away. I don't know where. They said it was for protection." He changed lanes and began to pick up speed.

"Were they afraid I would hurt her?" I asked in a small voice.

"No," Uncle Edmund said very gently. His hand darted out and gave my wrist a quick squeeze. "It was the other way around. They were afraid she would hurt you."

ONCE I'D GOTTEN MY car, once I'd driven it safely back to the Valley, I went right back to Uncle Edmund and Aunt Aggie's house. I spent the rest of the morning playing video games with Norbert in the basement. We didn't discuss anything. Norbert did his best to respect my desire for silence. It wasn't until after Aunt Aggie brought down pizza for lunch, and after we had washed it back with sodas from the little fridge, that my cousin couldn't take it any longer. "What now?" he burst out.

I'd sent Sky a text the night before. He'd never responded. I knew what I had to do.

"Now we go to back to my dad's house."

Norbert frowned. "Why?"

"Because my dad knows a lot about succubi."

"All the succubi we know are dead."

"True." I nodded. "But it turns out there are crazier things out there than succubi."

"Like what?"

"Like . . . the Abomination."

BY THE TIME WE'D parked ourselves among the stacks of boxes in my dad's upstairs study, I'd finished unloading everything to Norbert—all the things about the dark angel guy and Sky's betrayal, plus my own mysterious starring role in my epic family drama. I'd expected a big reaction.

I didn't get one.

Norbert was shockingly chill. He didn't even freak out upon learning that his aunt had allegedly been a member of an ancient, powerful race and that she—along with six others—had betrayed her kind. I mean, *our* kind.

He was all business.

"First things first," he said.

"Torch the place?" I suggested.

"I was thinking more along the lines of hacking into Uncle Lewis's network."

"That probably makes more sense." I allowed my eyes to travel around my dad's study. I hadn't set foot inside it in over two years, but everything was exactly how I remembered. Big carved worktable. A wall clock with hieroglyphics in place of numbers. A low bench made of amber, the shape of a skeleton suspended in its depths. I remembered being little and tracing its outline against the surface of the bench while my dad worked. He had told me it was a bat, but now that I was looking at it through more grown-up eyes, I could see that it had a double set of wings.

Like Corabelle's double tongue.

Norbert fired up my father's old desktop computer and started tapping away. "Do you want to check the book-case?"

I tore my eyes away from the bench. "Sure. What am I looking for?"

"I don't know. A family tree would be helpful."

I crossed to the shelves and started browsing. The books were old and dusty, and most titles seemed to relate to the earth: *Precambrian Mountain Ranges . . . Icelandic Hotspot . . . Weather Trends of the High Middle Ages . . .*

Norbert made a clucking sound.

"You got something?" I asked him.

"I'm almost in, but there's a block. I need a password."

"That could be anything."

"I know." Norbert peered at the computer screen. "It's more protected than I thought. I can't get past this prompt."

I turned away from the bookshelf. We were screwed. I didn't know the first concert my dad went to, or even his mother's birth name.

"It's weird, though, because it's not a question. It's a hint. He must have picked it himself. It's a word. One word."

I was almost afraid to ask. "What is it?"

Norbert looked up at me. "Regret."

What else? I felt a flash of anger. Regret was a luxury. It wasn't something my father should have been indulging in. Not when he had made the choice to run out on his family. Regret *that*, asshole.

Regret *me*.

"Try *family*," I said.

Tap-tap-tap. "Nope." Norbert hit a few more keys. "And not your name either. Or your mom's. Should I try birthdays?"

"Sure . . . No. Not birthdays. I know what he regrets. Try this." I paused for a second before I said it. "Rosemary."

Norbert thwacked some keys. He beamed up at me. "I'm in!"

ODDLY, THERE WASN'T A whole lot on succubi in the files. There was a whole lot more about creatures I'd never heard of. Creatures called the Elem.

According to my father's files, the Elem once ruled the world. They were like humans, but faster and stronger, with all kinds of crazy powers at their disposal. They were pretty much in charge of all the other creatures. Creatures like succubi.

But like all empires, theirs couldn't last forever. No empire can.

Just ask the Romans.

From what Norbert and I could discern from my father's notes, it looked like the Elem had *known* their rule was about to come to an end (which had to suck), so they'd started squabbling about what to do. They split into two factions. One wanted to become a part of the world that was coming, and the other wanted to fight against it. The two sides went to war, and you can pretty much guess what happened: whole cities turned to dust, massive calamities, things like that. At the end of the day, the leaders of both camps were forced to surrender. They got together and made a pact (or rather, a *Pact*): everyone would go to sleep—a special, magical sleep—rather than allow the world to be torn apart.

Norbert squinted at the screen. "It says the Elem 'crawled into the bones of the earth.'"

"What does that mean, 'bones of the earth'?"

He shrugged. "You got me."

I flashed back to the rooftop and what Corabelle had said to me. My mother hadn't fallen asleep with her kind. She and the other six traitors had stayed awake, and now others were awakening too.

"Corabelle," I said out loud.

"Huh?"

"Corabelle said she'd been awakened . . ."

But that didn't make sense. Corabelle was a succubus, not an Elem. I returned to the screen. "All evidence of their existence was erased from the world," I read aloud before looking over at Norbert again. "Okay, that's wrong. We *know* all evidence wasn't erased because, besides the monsters we keep tripping over, everyone keeps talking about keys and bridges."

Norbert shrugged again, peering at the screen. "Maybe it's like wiping a kitchen counter. It might look like you got everything. You might even have used a spray bottle, but you always miss a crumb or two. Maybe a piece sticks in the grout or gets stuck in a corner somewhere. A splash of milk dries before anyone can clean it, and the residue is still there, nearly invisible. Stuff sticks around."

I swatted his arm. "That's a lot to get from Dad's file."

"I'm extrapolating."

I started to pace around the cluttered room, my mind racing again, a familiar heat rising somewhere inside my chest. "The Pact was broken. And the new world has to be _our_ world. So do you think that guy on the roof was an Elem? One of the original seven hidden Elem? If so, he would have known my mother." I waited for my cousin to agree with me, but when I looked over at him, he was frozen. "Norb?"

He stared at the screen.

"Norbert!"

His face had gone pale. "They set a trap for the seven who didn't sleep." He quoted the words as they formed in my head, lifted verbatim from the terrifying memory of that _thing_ in Misty's lair: _"The seven lied and one of them died."_

"Norbert." I whispered.

"Jillian, there's more," he whispered back.

Of course there was more.

"There was a law," he said. And then he spit it out in one fast breath: "A-law-decreeing-separation-between-worlds."

"What does that even—" I started to ask, and then stopped.

Click.

The puzzle pieces came together with a sickening lurch.

I stared at Norbert. "Someone broke that law. Two some-ones. An Elem and a human."

Norbert stood and stepped toward me, unsure of what to do. I knew he wanted to hug me. But he also knew I didn't want to be hugged. "You were that first child. When you were born, the trap was sprung. The doors opened for the old world to come back."

"Corabelle was right. It *is* my fault." Somehow, I squeezed the words out past the horror that rose up in my throat, strangling any hope for light at the end of this very dark tunnel. "When I was born, the monsters came."

TWENTY-EIGHT

Norbert finally went home after leaving a voice mail for Sky. I also tried to call him several times but didn't hear back until early evening. Until then, I was left alone with my thoughts. The ones that were all about unleashing hell, for starters. And also the ones about the con man whose biggest, longest con had been on his own daughter. And about Rosemary. But mostly they were about Sky, the one puzzle piece that still refused to fit.

At 7:15, Sky texted, asking me to meet him.

I immediately called Norbert.

"Meet him," Norbert said.

"Really? Do you want to come?"

He laughed gently. "No, you got this one. But you know that you're not alone now, right, Jilly Willy?"

I hung up before he could get sappier.

LA-96C, ALSO KNOWN AS the Nike missile site, is a hiking destination off Mulholland Drive above Encino. Technically speaking, it really should be known as an *anti*missile site, since its purpose during the Cold War was to detect hostile aircraft.

I wished it could detect all things that were hostile.

I'd been there once before, so I was familiar with the layout. I parked on the dirt track near the entrance and, ignoring the signs that the area was closed after sunset, climbed over a yellow gate and onto the trail. I used my (now fully charged) phone to light the way. I had downloaded a flashlight app, which was surprisingly bright.

With its help, I reached the radar tower in less than ten minutes of silent walking. I paused for a moment at the base. A crooked ramp led up into the darkness.

Halfway up, I saw that Sky was already there, standing in the center of the platform on top. When he heard me, he flashed his own phone to light my way.

"I should have met you in the parking lot," he said. "It would have been the gentlemanly thing to do."

"That's never been your strong suit," I said, walking past him to the edge of the platform. As I set my hands upon the chest-level railing, I had a brief flashback to the last time I had been this high above the ground with my hands on a scabby metal bar. That time, someone had died. I shook off the memory and turned to Sky. Of course he was even more angular and messy and beautiful by starlight.

"Why here?" I asked him.

Sky set his hands on my shoulders and gently turned me back to face the way I had been looking, out over the Los Angeles Basin, where millions of lights twinkled up at us, the dark silhouette of the mountain ranges beyond. "Because this is your city," he told me. "Because it's

mystifying and dangerous, but it's also beautiful and com-
plicated." He wrapped his arms around me from behind
and tucked his face down close to my ear. "Like you," he
whispered.

If I had been a normal girl with a normal life, the
moment would have been perfect. I would have spun
around in the circle of Sky's arms. I would have risen up
on tiptoes to kiss him. This would have become our pre-
ferred spot for make-out sessions. Maybe I would have
changed my online status to "in a relationship."

But I wasn't a normal girl. I was the daughter of an
ancient betrayer. And my life wasn't normal because the
boy who liked me was also the boy who had deceived me.

I pulled away and took a step backward, putting distance
between our two bodies. "Tell me about the obituary."

"I will. I promise. But I want you to know something."
Sky smiled the most gentle, saddest of smiles. "I have no
regrets about any of this."

Well, that makes one of us.

"In that first moment by your locker, the whole world
opened up," he continued. "Before, I didn't really believe
in anything, and now, everything is possible."

I wanted to cry, but I didn't know why. "Say it," I whispered. "Please just tell me."

"Will you believe me?"

I registered the pain in his eyes, but I still told him the
truth. "Probably not."

"Then why are you here?"

"Because I want to hear it anyway."

Sky nodded. He ran his fingers through his hair, making

it messier than usual. He took a deep breath and let it out slowly, like he was releasing more than air. Then he pulled a tablet out of his jacket's interior pocket, turned it on, and tilted it toward me.

On the screen was a photo of a taffy-yellow two-story home. "What am I looking at?"

"My house in San Francisco. It's three blocks from the bay." Sky swiped a finger across the tablet, and a cocker spaniel came into view. It was lounging on a rug in front of a fireplace. Nearby, a tabby kitten was caught midlick, cleaning its paw. Sky pointed to the dog. "That's Odie. The cat is Lars."

"Cute." I wasn't sure why I was getting a tour of Sky's personal life, but I figured it was best to play along.

Sky swiped again, and now a middle-aged couple smiled at me from a picnic bench. "Dad's a partner at an insurance company and Mom's an architect. And this was me, last year." It was a picture of Sky himself, lying on a queen-sized bed in the middle of a messy room. He was asleep, one arm draped over his face. He was wearing . . .

"A letter jacket?"

"Varsity soccer. Team captain." Sky's smile widened into one that was more familiar. "Oh, you would have hated me. I made good grades in everything except math. I fiddled around with a guitar. Sometimes I partied."

"You were a jock." I shook my head. "That's almost as weird as finding out the cheerleader was a succubus."

"Right, but it all changed last spring." Sky's grin fell away. My stomach muscles tightened.

"What happened?"

fake

"I was asleep." Sky pointed to the photo of himself. "But in the middle of the night, something woke me up. I don't know how because I don't remember a sound, but suddenly I was awake, and there was a shadow standing over my bed. It should have been super creepy . . ." He paused, remembering. "I mean, it *was* creepy, but then the shadow started talking in this delicate, silvery voice, and suddenly it wasn't scary anymore. It was just . . . weird. The shadow said, 'I'm not really here.'" Sky shook his head. "I guess I should have yelled for my parents or something, but its voice was so fragile, and it chose its words so carefully. I didn't feel like I was in danger."

I had a hard time believing I would feel so safe with a stranger looming over me in my sleep, but who knows? Crazier things had happened in the last week.

"It leaned close to me," Sky continued. "Close enough that I should have been able to feel its breath when it whispered in my ear, but I couldn't. I couldn't feel anything. All I could hear was what it said. 'You have to save the world.'"

I must have made a tiny sound, because Sky stopped talking and turned to look at me.

"What?"

Out of habit, I was about to make a snarky comment—*Delusions of grandeur, much?*—but the look on Sky's face made me decide against it. "Nothing."

"The shadow said, 'There is someone who must be protected. If she dies, so will the world.'" He looked at me again. "Which I know sounds nuts. It sounded nuts at the time too. But when I heard it . . . that's when I felt like I was finally all the way awake, because I suddenly had all these questions. I think I said something, like 'What?' or 'Huh?' and the shadow said, 'You have to protect her.'"

My heart lurched. I flashed back to the empty parking lot, to the moment right after Sky kissed me and right before we went searching for the succubus lair. He had said it to me then. *All I want to do is protect you.* I wanted to remind Sky of that moment, but he was still talking. Still telling me his story.

Still telling me *our* story.

"The shadow said I was being sent into a time that didn't exist yet. It said that I had to make sure that it never would, because if it came to pass, our world would end." Sky paused. "That was the phrasing. 'Your world will end.'"

"Our world." I said it out loud. What I didn't tell Sky was what Corabelle had called my mother. *Destroyer of worlds.*

"I tried to get more information," Sky told me. "I asked, 'Why *me?*' and the shadow said it saw the paths of the future and that they're always twisting and changing, but that when it saw *hers*—"

"Hers," I repeated numbly.

"Yeah, *now* I know it was talking about you," Sky said. "But at the time, I asked the shadow who it meant, and it was really sketchy about answering. It kept saying things like 'Her' and 'She who must be protected.' I told it that I got that part, and I just wanted to know what we *call* the person who must be protected. The shadow said, 'We call her by her name,' and I said, 'Right, that's the part I'm trying to get. What's her name?'" Sky gave me a wry smile. "It told me to stop interrupting. I actually apologized, if you can believe that. Anyway, then it told me that when it looked into the future, it saw *me* on *your* paths."

Sky's tablet suddenly turned itself off, because we hadn't been using it. As my eyes readjusted to the starlight, he slid the tablet back into his jacket and looked down at me. "It said that it saw me on your good paths. On the happy ones. It said that sometimes I meet you in a room filled with books, and sometimes over a glass of ruby liquid. It had seen me stumble into you in a patch of open grass, and it had seen us find each other while walking over warm sand." He gazed down at me. "It said that the futures that bring you to me are all the ones where you are happy and strong and filled with light."

I knew I wasn't any of those things. I was scared and sad and filled with confusion. None of this made sense. "What was so bad about the other future, the one you had to stop?"

"I asked it the same thing," Sky told me. "The shadow said that it would show me. It waved its hand over my head. I started to reach out, to try and grab it, but I was suddenly tired like I hadn't slept in a month. Like it *did* something to me. I tried to keep my eyes open, but I couldn't. Everything faded to black, and as I fell asleep, the shadow said, 'Save her. Save her and you save the world.'"

"So you *were* dreaming?" I asked him. "You were asleep the whole time?"

"No, *then* I started dreaming," Sky told me. "I could tell because everything was weird and twisty and blurry like in a dream. I was outside a church. A small one with wooden doors. A handful of mourners were walking in. I could tell they were in mourning because everyone was wearing black, and some of them were crying. I started to follow them in, but—because it was a dream and you know how sometimes this happens in dreams—suddenly I just *was* in. It was the church's lobby, I guess. There weren't that many people inside, but . . ." Sky trailed off for a moment, remembering.

"What?" My voice trembled when I said the word.

"It seemed like more. It seemed like thousands. Or millions, even. I could *feel* their sadness. It was heavy and awful, like the entire world was crying. And there I was, in the middle of all that private grief. Feeling it all around me, but not understanding . . . until I saw it. Over by the entrance to the sanctuary, there was a bulletin board on a stand. I . . ." He paused, searching for a word. "I *ghosted* over to it. That's what it felt like when I moved around, like I was a ghost. It didn't seem like anyone could see me."

"What was on the bulletin board?"

Sky gazed at me for a moment before answering. "Someone had decorated the edges with rose petals and leaves, and in the very middle of the board, there was an obituary."

My lips went cold. Sky kept talking.

"I took a step closer so I could read it, but everything was still all blurry and watery around me. Before my eyes could focus, someone shouted at me. Someone across the lobby. They yelled, 'Wake up!' and I knew I'd been found out. Someone *knew* I didn't belong. There were footsteps pounding toward me, and everything started to dissolve. The whole church was going away. The air shimmered and I could hear the rain against my bedroom window at home. I knew I had to do *something* to hold on because I hadn't figured out who the shadow wanted me to save. So I lurched forward, grabbing at the obituary . . ."

"And you got it." The words managed to escape from between my frozen lips. "You got the obituary."

"Only half of it," Sky told me. "A hand grabbed my shoulder, but I already had the paper in my hand. It ripped away from the bulletin board, and everything started to fade. All the shouting and crying grew dimmer and then evaporated into nothing at all. I was back in my bedroom. I had been gone—or asleep or whatever—for most of the rest of the night, because it was very, very early morning. Light was just beginning to come through the blinds, and the shadow was still there. For just a second, it was still there. And it wasn't a shadow anymore. It was a girl."

"A girl?" I said.

"She disappeared into thin air," Sky told me. "Just . . . vanished. I probably would have thought it had all been a dream—a regular, normal dream—except for two things. The first was the scratch on my left shoulder blade, where someone had grabbed me. Even that I could have explained away, like maybe I did it to myself while dreaming."

"But you still had my obituary." It came out as a statement, not a question.

"Yes," said Sky. "It came from my dream of the future. It

was solid and it was real, and when I did an online search for you, I found your dad's website."

"So you're not a crazy longtime fan of my father," I said slowly, as the last of my anger slid away.

"I'd never even heard of him until I searched for your name online," said Sky. "But once I realized he was a professor of the occult, I knew I had to learn as much about that stuff as I possibly could. So I watched his videos, and I ordered his books, and then I researched every other paranormal expert I could find."

"That's why you know so much about succubi," I murmured.

"Yeah, and about you."

I cocked my head at him. "Then why put the obituary in my locker? Why not just hand it over to begin with, and save me the heartache and the torture and all of it?"

"Would you have bought it?" Sky asked. "Would you have believed that the new dude in school just happened to possess a partial copy of your obituary that came from the future? Would you have taken it seriously?"

I opened my mouth, and closed it. "Well . . . probably not." I considered. "What did she look like?"

Sky frowned. "Who?"

"The shadow." I was curious, but mostly I was trying to buy time while I sorted through my thoughts and feelings.

"I was just blinking awake, and she was gone so fast. I didn't get a really good look, but . . . I can still picture her eyes."

My mouth went dry. "Why? What about her eyes?"

"They didn't have pupils," said Sky. "They were white, like her hair."

That's when I knew for sure that Sky was telling the truth.

"Rosemary," I said. "That was my sister, Rosemary."

TWENTY-NINE

On Friday morning, I took Norbert to school early. I had stayed over at his house again because, although I didn't plan on making it a regular habit, I figured a few nights would help defuse my aunt and uncle's great desire to watch over me.

Besides, it was kind of nice. Uncle Edmund made a delicious lasagna, and my aunt's homemade brownies were to die for, plus Norbert taught me how to play contract rummy. It felt safe there. Nice.

Normal.

Best of all, we didn't talk about any of it.

Until Aunt Aggie cornered me before I could get to my car where Norbert was waiting patiently in the passenger seat. She pulled me off to the side of the porch and peered into my eyes. We were about the same height. I had never noticed that before.

"It's not your fault," Aunt Aggie said.

I blinked, not sure which part she was talking about or how much she knew.

"Rosemary," my aunt clarified. "It's not your fault they sent her away. I offered to take her back to North Carolina with us, but your mom said she had to go further than that. Things were happening in the house, and your mother was afraid for both of you."

My heart beat faster. "What kind of things?"

"Sounds, mostly. Like whispers in the air."

I stared at her. "You said 'mostly.' What else?"

"Oh, Jillian, it sounds so crazy when I say it out loud." She shook her head, giving me a rueful smile. "Lights went out, and things would fall, and once—" She stopped.

I swallowed hard. "What? Say it."

"Her crib burst into flames." My aunt reached out to touch the arm she wasn't holding. "Rosemary was fine but your parents were scared. For both of you."

"Where did she go?" My lips were numb, but somehow I got the words out through them.

"I don't know, honey, but I can tell you that on our visit, I saw the two of you together. Rosemary was in this little basket on the living room floor, waving her hands and feet around. You toddled over and peeked at her, and she looked straight at you. It was the first time I thought maybe she could see after all. Your mom ran over to pull you away, but your dad stopped her. He said sisters should get to know each other."

The numbness had descended to my throat, becoming an iceberg of pain. I was afraid that if I swallowed again, it would shatter into liquid, and there would be only one place for the water to escape. My eyes.

Aunt Aggie's grip on my other arm tightened. "Rosemary

fake

smiled when she saw you," she told me. "That time and every time you came near, she would smile. Sometimes you babbled at her, and sometimes you touched her, but every time—every single time when we were there—you made that baby smile. Rosemary loved you. You have a sister somewhere and she loves you."

The sun came out. The iceberg floated away and melted. "Thank you," I said. "Thank you for telling me."

Then, for the first time ever, I initiated one of Aunt Aggie's angel-love hugs.

AT SCHOOL, I FOUND Sky surrounded by lilac bushes, on the bench where Corabelle had first told us about Todd Harmon. I sat down beside him, breathed in the scent of the flowers, and gazed into those amazing green eyes. He reached for my hand, and I allowed him to take it. Then I said the three most difficult words I had ever spoken in my life.

"No more kissing."

Sky frowned. "You mean at school, right? No more kissing at school."

"Yes."

He looked relieved. "Good, because at first I thought—"

"Or at home or in cars or succubus night clubs or on benches. Especially not on benches."

"Jillian." He scooted closer to me and leaned in, like maybe his nearness would change my mind. It came awfully close to doing so. "I told you the truth. I told you everything."

"I know. I believe you. And that's why we can't be together."

Sky released my hand, looking bewildered. "I don't understand."

"You didn't come here for me," I said, the hurt washing up and over me like it had late the night before when I'd made the realization. "You came for a *dream* of me."

"But the dream was *real.* We are meant for each other. Your happiest futures all lead to me." Lines appeared around his eyes and he looked sad. Confused. "Jillian, we are *supposed* to be together. It's fate, like I've been telling you all along."

"Sky . . ." I paused, swallowing back the lump in my throat. This was even harder than I'd thought it would be, and I had thought it would be epically hard. "You don't know me."

"Yes I do!"

"No, you know information that you found online, and we had a couple days of succubus hunting together, and you want to protect me so you can save the world, because for some unfathomable reason, I matter or—"

"Of course you matter."

"—or at least my missing sister thinks I do. That's not *knowing* me."

"I'm *getting* to know you," Sky argued. "It's what I said I wanted at the very beginning. Knowing you, *really* knowing you . . . that part will come."

"I agree."

"You do?" His green eyes looked hopeful, and my heart clenched, aching with the pain of losing him. But it was better than losing myself *into* him.

"That's why we can't rush it. You want to save the world, right?"

"Right."

"Then let's do that first. Let's find Rosemary. Let's figure out what the obituary meant. Let's make sure it doesn't come true. Let's find the bridge and burn it like my mom said, so the armies can't cross over. Let's do all *that* stuff together." I was so intent on making him understand that I didn't realize I had caught his hand again until his hard, smooth fingers were sliding between my own. When I spoke again, my voice trembled. "You were right, Sky. You were right the whole time. There *are* bigger, scarier things out there, and now we are two of the very few people in the world who know they exist. That has to come first."

Sky's gaze danced across my face for a moment before he slowly nodded. "You're saying fate can wait."

"I'm saying kissing can wait."

The part I didn't say out loud was that it was still about trust. It wasn't that I didn't trust Sky Ramsey to be truthful. For all of Corabelle's dark delusions, she had been right about one thing: the human heart was the weakest part of us. Sky cared about me because the dream had told him that he *had* to care about me. But until he came to me in his own way, on his own terms, it didn't mean what it should mean. It didn't count the same way. It didn't really count at all.

"We can still hang out together," I told him. "Just no—"

"No kissing." He completed the sentence with a rueful smile.

"Right." I reached into the side pocket of my backpack

and pulled out the email I had printed the night before. "Besides, kissing takes time. We're not going to have enough minutes in the day for a bunch of time-wasting kissing."

Sky eyed the paper. "Why?"

"Because we got a new case."

Sky's eyes darted back up to mine. *"We?"*

"Yeah." I waggled my eyebrows at him. "Unless you're not interested in being a part of Umbra. Unless you don't want to work with me."

He made a grab for the paper, but I held it behind my back. "Hold on. I need to hear you say it."

"It."

"So funny." I shook my head at him. "No, really. Repeat after me: I, Sky Ramsey, do solemnly swear to partner with Jillian on all things Umbra."

"I, Sky Ramsey, do solemnly swear to partner with Jillian on all things Umbra even though I still want to kiss her."

I made a face at him and kept going. "And to always tell her the truth about everything, past and present."

"And to always tell her the truth about everything, past and present . . ." Sky leaned close to me. "And future."

"Good point. Also I promise to do whatever she says at all times and in all—"

"In your dreams," said Sky, nudging me.

"Hey, you're the one with the dreams," I told him with a return nudge. We sat there for a moment, grinning at each other, and then I brandished the paper. "So don't you want to hear about our new case?"

"Let me guess. Is it another succubus?"

fake (above CADE)

"Better."

"Better than a succubus?" Sky considered. "A vampire? Ghost? Troll?" I shook my head after each guess. "An orc?"

"Please. There's no such thing as an orc."

"Give me a hint."

"Remember the week we just had."

I watched him contemplate and fought back the desire to touch his streaked blond hair. There would be time for that after we knew each other better. "Think hard heads," I said. "Anger issues."

"Asterions . . ." Sky said slowly. "We do know there are at least two of them hanging around Los Angeles."

"Bingo."

Sky reached out again, and this time, I let him take the paper from me. I watched his eyes move back and forth across it before widening and lifting to meet my own. "Jillian," he said in a whisper. "This isn't a case *about* a descendant of Asterion."

"I know." I felt the smile blossom across my face, all at once exhilarated and fascinated and—to be one hundred percent honest—a little bit scared. "It's a case request *from* one."

We stared at each other for a moment, and then Sky grabbed my hand with his own and pumped it vigorously. "Let's do it."

"All right, partner."

AT LUNCHTIME, AS USUAL, I spotted Norbert sitting in the cafeteria with his new freshmen buddies. We waved at each other and I headed outside. But I'd made a resolution. For the first time ever, I wasn't going to lose myself in the horde of screen-obsessed students on the front lawn or eat lunch alone on the hood of my car.

I was going to seek someone out.

Laura was leaning against a magnolia tree on the edge of campus—not far from the bird-poop bench where it had all started—when I plopped down beside her. "Okay to sit here?"

Laura looked startled. More than startled. She jerked upright with a little squeal, nearly knocking over her carton of chocolate milk.

"Sorry," she whispered. "I wasn't expecting anyone."

"So I can sit here?"

She blinked, and then nodded. "Yes. Yes, of course you can. Please, have a seat."

It seemed rude to mention that I had already done so. And I was no longer going to be rude. At least, not if I could help it. I dug my spork into the cafeteria manicotti and held it up for a moment, letting it cool. "Did I miss anything important in class yesterday?"

Laura paused, waiting for a catch. I watched it slowly dawn on her that there wasn't one. I was just trying to be a normal girl talking to another normal girl.

"Not really," she said. "Except Henry got in trouble for talking dirty. Something about Helen of Troy and a swan."

"Sorry I missed that." I popped the bite into my mouth and grinned through the tomato and starch and cheese.

She laughed. "Also, Mr. Lowe is going to have us team up on an epic hero project. Do you want to be in my group?"

"Yeah." I swallowed my bite and nodded at the same time. "I'm in."

"Great," said Laura. "I'll email you the notes."

And just like that, I had a friend.

THE REST OF THE day was uneventful—in the good way—and that afternoon, I drove to the Los Angeles Department of Water and Power to pay my electric bill. After everything I'd been through, it felt like an accomplishment.

When I got back to my father's house—my house—and unlocked the front door, I hesitated a moment. This was the place where my sister had taken her first breaths. Where my mother had taken her last. This was a place of secrets and of regrets and, hopefully, of new beginnings and questions answered.

I reached in and slid my hand up the wall next to the door, turning on the lights. Then I did something I hadn't done in months and months.

I went inside and yanked up the window shades.

Sunlight flooded in, banishing the shadows and washing the room in gold. Maybe I only had six months to live, or maybe ahead of me lay years and years of life. Either way, I had learned a very important lesson.

The world didn't have to be so dark.

EPILOGUE

I told Norbert and Sky not to come over to my father's house until noon on Saturday, so everyone could have a chance to sleep in and recover from everything we'd been through. It was a good plan, except that I woke up at the same time I did on weekdays. That's why I went over early, and why I was all alone, digging through my father's stuff in the living room, when it happened.

I had just opened a battered leather satchel and found an empty folder labeled BRIDGE when the voice interrupted my search. It was a voice that said my name. A familiar voice that immediately soaked me in rage, in longing, in regret. I looked up at the figure standing in the doorway, and even though I knew—I *knew*—I should throw things, scream, run away . . .

. . . old habits die hard. As I had learned over and over and over that week, the head knows better but the heart betrays.

So instead of shrieking or fleeing, I did the exact opposite. I rose to my feet, and I ran straight toward the man standing in the doorway. I flung my arms around him, tears spilling, not knowing what the words would be until after they'd tumbled from my mouth.

"Daddy, you came home."

ACKNOWLEDGMENTS

Here's the thing: when there's a sex demon in your book, you simply cannot dedicate that book to your children. Or your parents. Or even to your husband because it's just weird, and readers might wonder about your personal life. You CAN, however, dedicate it to the people with whom you once TALKED about sex. The ones who have known you in the most unique way, in the way that has its own language, its own history, its own angels and demons; a way that spans childhood to adulthood. Especially if the book also features—besides sex demons—a protagonist who really, really wants to know her sister. And if you're already lucky enough—in REAL LIFE—to really, really know your three very smart, very cool, very awesome sisters . . .

That's why the dedication. Because I have the smartest, coolest, most awesome sisters.

And also because—sex demon.

Now for some gratitude.

Because I'm a debut author and we are known to have long lists of acknowledgments, I might as well milk it because THE FIRST BOOK ONLY HAPPENS ONCE. Therefore, thank you so very much to the following horde of people:

My indefatigable, passionate, dedicated, all-the-good-adjectives book agent: Lisa Gallagher. I could not ask for a better partner. I'm consistently thrilled and amazed and happily startled by how this works. To a zillion more . . .

The biggest of wet sloppy thanks to Dan Ehrenhaft who took a half-written, raw, messy pile of words and guided it into a story that makes me proud. Working with him was a privilege and a joy, especially those times when one of us got extra excited and went all SHOUTY-CAPS in an email. I am wildly grateful to have been found by him.

Everyone on the Soho Teen dream team who helped this become a real, live book: Bronwen Hruska, Meredith Barnes, Janine Agro, Rachel Kowal, and Amara Hoshijo.

Jennifer Pooley for being an actual fairy godmother. Champagne o'clock!

Nina Berry who was willing to read all the chapters as fast as I could write when I was under a deadline, and who also was not afraid to say the things that needed to be said.

Elise Allen for explaining how it works in Book-Landia.

Nicole Maggi, Lizzie Andrews, Anne Van, Romina Russell, Will Frank—for being the first to read and rip apart.

David Furr who made me feel pretty when he took my headshots.

fake

Wendi Gu at Sanford J. Greenburger Associates for her early read and enthusiasm.

Kelly Trussell, Sally Schultheiss, Brendalyn Richard, Hillary Felder, Laurie Peebler, and all the other friends who help just because I ask. Because we are parents, home owners, women—and sometimes we need an extra person to watch the kids or feed the dogs or just listen. And especially Melanie Snell who is the heart and soul of my freaking village.

Ed Pilkington—for long ago telling me what I didn't yet believe: that I was a writer—and to Michael Stokes for showing me how.

The writing and support staff of *Grey's Anatomy*, season 11. Guys—you teach me every day and inspire me more than you know. Seriously, all of you. You have no idea. You're all wonderful writers and—so much more importantly—beautiful humans.

Matt Horwitz, Rina Brannen, Tom Collier—who are so supportive and loving when I take a little time to follow my heart into a book. I seriously don't know how I lucked into the best screenwriting reps in the world.

And mostly—Josh. Jake. Sam. For all the best parts of life and love.